## "I want to explore this attraction between us," Jake said

"You can't deny it exists," he continued. With his hands wrapped in Brianne's hair, he brought his fingers to her cheek and stroked slowly, methodically, over her skin. "I know *I* feel it every time we're together. Don't you?"

He leaned in closer. Their breaths mingled and a hint of peppermint reached her nose, a scent she'd never found arousing. Until now. Brianne's heart hammered out a rapid beat in her chest.

"We're living together, working together.... It could get messy," she said, desperately trying to keep her desire at bay.

"Or it could be amazing," Jake countered.

"I'm not in the market for a serious relationship right now," she said, still fighting to make him see reason. Although by his expression, she knew her attempts were falling on deaf ears. Jake wouldn't be put off.

"I'm not, either," he said, bringing his lips even closer. "Brianne, Brianne... We want the same things—each other and a short-term affair. And we need each other. I need your personal expertise—and I need you in my bed." He paused. "And if you're honest with yourself, you'll admit you need it, too...."

Dear Reader,

Harlequin Blaze is a supersexy new series. If you like love stories with a strong sexual edge, then this is the line for you! The books are fun and flirtatious, the heroes are hot and outrageous. Blaze is a series for the woman who wants *more* in her reading pleasure....

This month, *USA Today* bestselling author JoAnn Ross brings you #5 *Thirty Nights,* a provocative story about a man who wants a woman for only thirty nights of sheer pleasure. Then popular Kimberly Raye poses the question of what women really expect in a man, in the sizzling #6 *The Pleasure Principle.* Talented Candace Schuler delivers #7 *Uninhibited,* a hot story with two fiery protagonists who have few inhibitions—about each other! Carly Phillips rounds out the month with another SEXY CITY NIGHTS story set in New York—where the heat definitely escalates after dark...

Look for four Blaze books every month at your favorite bookstore. And check us out online at eHarlequin.com and tryblaze.com.

Enjoy!

Birgit Davis-Todd
Senior Editor & Editorial Coordinator
Harlequin Blaze

# BODY HEAT

*Carly Phillips*

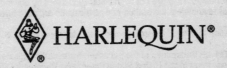

TORONTO • NEW YORK • LONDON
AMSTERDAM • PARIS • SYDNEY • HAMBURG
STOCKHOLM • ATHENS • TOKYO • MILAN • MADRID
PRAGUE • WARSAW • BUDAPEST • AUCKLAND

ISBN 0-373-79012-0

BODY HEAT

**Printed in U.S.A.**

# A NOTE FROM THE AUTHOR...

New York City—sizzling by day, decadent by night. There's no better place for fantasies to come true.... That's something Brianne Nelson and Jake Lowell discover as they spend every night of the long, hot summer together. An agreed-upon affair quickly escalates until the fantasy is no longer enough and only forever will do. But how can the relationship last when Jake's deceit brings danger to their door?

Welcome to the second month of Blaze, Harlequin's hottest new line. I'm proud and excited to be a part of the launch of this sizzling new series, and the second book in the SEXY CITY NIGHTS miniseries. Let me know if I'm making your reading fantasies come true. You can write to me at: P.O. Box 483, Purchase, NY 10577. Or check out my Web site at www.carlyphillips.com.

In the meantime, sit back and feel the heat....

Carly Phillips

## Books by Carly Phillips

### HARLEQUIN TEMPTATION
775—SIMPLY SINFUL
779—SIMPLY SCANDALOUS
815—SIMPLY SENSUAL
836—SECRET FANTASY

To my Park Lane friends—
Jill Baker, Giselle Gerson, Marcie Klein, Ilyssa Marks,
Abby Mendelsohn and Allison Tannenbaum.
I doubt you understand my writing obsession, but you're
there for me—even when you don't see or hear from me
for weeks on end. And to Sharon Stein, not only a
good friend, but my ultimate fan. Thanks for being so
wonderful in good times and bad. I love you all.

## Acknowledgment

A special thanks to Lynda Sue Cooper
for her never-ending gushing about my first book, *Brazen*,
and for her unlimited knowledge about the police force.
Any mistakes are mine alone.

# 1

___

THE DAYS WERE HOT but, thanks to her, his nights were even hotter. He welcomed the mixture of anticipation and desire that rushed through him as he looked around The Sidewalk Café. As he looked for *her*.

Jake Lowell clasped his hand around a chilled glass of ice water. The condensation left his palm cold and wet, in stark contrast to the New York City heat and humidity pulsing around him. In opposition to the inferno raging inside him. Nothing could extinguish the flame she'd ignited.

He leaned forward in the wrought-iron seat, shifting, trying to find a comfortable position for his back against the hard metal, one that wouldn't put pressure on his left shoulder and the injury that had finally begun to heal. He shifted again, and pain shot through his upper body. Damn fancy chair. Outdoor cafés with sissy drinks weren't his thing, they were his sister's. But ever since he'd come here for the first time, ever since he'd taken a look at the sexy waitress with the compelling gaze, he'd forced himself to endure.

Jake glanced around, but the woman who starred in his fantasies was nowhere to be found.

Only a few couples graced the outdoor section of the restaurant. He looked at his watch. Typical of his sister, Rina, she was already fifteen minutes late. After a childhood of sharing one bathroom with a teenage girl, he'd become used to waiting for her; he'd be shocked if she showed up on time. But with the guy who shot Jake wandering the street, Rina's lateness—typical or not—made him wary.

He took in the empty street once more, then turned toward the inside of the nearly empty restaurant and bar, reminding himself that the scum was now living a so-called clean life and that his sister was safe. He headed inside, figuring he'd wait for Rina in front of the television set and a good Yankee game.

That was when he saw *her*—his vision in white jeans and a black tank top with an apron tied around her waist. She stood by the bar, a bottle of water in hand. Her auburn hair had been pulled back in a pony-tail while stray strands resisted confinement and curled around a face with delicate, angelic features. More than lust or desire, it was the purity in her expression and the smile on her lips that lured him back to this place, to her, over and over again.

After reading an order off her pad, she shoved it into her pocket, and the bartender got busy mixing drinks. Jake rose from his seat and walked to the open sliding glass door that led to the inside of the restaurant. She leaned against the wall and glanced around—looking for what, he didn't know. Then she tipped her head backward and ran the bottle over her forehead, down one cheek and then the next, until she finally eased it over her long neck.

As the bottle moved over her skin, he swallowed a groan. Her back arched and her breasts pushed against the black tank. Taut nipples teased both the fabric and his restraint. He ought to feel like a voyeur, yet her every sensual, seductive movement seemed as if it had been choreographed for his eyes only.

Though she was a stranger, he felt as if he knew her intimately, yet not intimately enough. Eyes shut tight, her shoulders dropped and her muscles relaxed. As the cold plastic touched bare skin, her long sigh echoed inside him. Whether aware or not, she'd aroused both his curiosity and his imagination.

What would she taste like? he wondered. Would he find her lips moist, her mouth flavored with mint? Or would she taste sweet, like the coffee drinks served here? And in the throes of passion would she meet his gaze or shut her eyes in expectation and pleasure? Just imagining making love to her had his body strung tight with need and his soul on fire. He took neither lightly.

Little had piqued his interest other than the incident that had sidelined him and taken down Frank Dickinson, his best friend and fellow detective, causing Jake to rethink his direction in life. But desire licked at him now, hotter and with more force than the bullet that had seared his skin.

Neon lights over the bar reflected off the droplets of water on her flesh. He wanted to taste her damp heat, to absorb it with his body. He broke into a sweat that had nothing to do with the heat wave outside. His hand had turned wet from the condensation on the glass, and he wiped his palm on jeans that had grown too tight.

She straightened and placed her bottle on the bar before glancing around the confines of the small restaurant. He held his breath, but she didn't look in his direction. Then she grabbed a napkin and blotted the glistening skin on her chest, patting downward to where droplets had probably dripped into the *V* of her cleavage, nestling between her full breasts.

Without warning, she turned and glanced his way. Her gaze met his and her eyes grew wide, not with horror but with surprise. Just as he thought, she hadn't known anyone was watching. But when the surprise wore off, she stared at him with more than a hint of interest in her expression.

It was an interest he recognized because she captivated him, too. The mutual attraction had been strong from the first. And over the past few weeks, the sizzling awareness had only grown stronger.

His sister had fed his interest, meeting him here in the evenings so he could get his fill. And *she'd* always been here, always waiting on tables in stations other than his. He didn't know why she hadn't approached him, only why he'd maintained the distance. Fantasy, he'd learned, always surpassed gritty reality.

But never had the current between them been as charged as it was tonight. Their connection was electric, so all-encompassing that his body throbbed with need and his mind soared with myriad possibilities— none of which he intended to act upon.

She still held his gaze, as if waiting for him to make the next move. Without breaking eye contact, he lifted his glass in silent acknowledgment. He expected her to turn away, to rebuff his subtle advance. She did neither. Instead she held his stare with a searing heat and bold curiosity he hadn't expected—until the bartender's arrival with her order severed the connection.

She glanced back at him once more before she crumpled the napkin and tossed it into the trash. Then she returned to business, taking orders and serving drinks. But the flush in her cheeks remained, testament to what had passed between them.

"Oh my God, Jake, I'm sorry." His sister's voice calling him brought him out of the sensual haze, though the sizzling in his veins remained.

Relieved Rina had showed up unharmed, he headed back to his table and settled himself into the uncomfortable seat. Though distracted, he tried to focus as she slid into the chair across from him. Her skin glistened from the humidity and her dark hair clung to her cheeks. She was no different from most rushed and overheated New Yorkers, yet her outfit distinguished her from the other mostly jean-wearing patrons of the café. All elegance, she appeared out of place in the casual atmosphere, but Rina being Rina, she failed to notice.

"I know I'm late. But Norton hates the heat," she said, talking about her Chinese sharpei. He was all wrinkles with a black tongue, a dog no self-respecting person would take out in public, but Jake had developed a soft spot for the pedigreed pooch.

He shook his head and laughed. "Money really has changed you, Ri." They'd grown up with a half-breed mutt that had wandered through the dirt and grime of the South Bronx. The dog had taken a nap one day by the front of their building and had stayed.

When Rina, a legal secretary, had met and married her boss, Jake had had his doubts about the man and the marriage. Who wouldn't question a guy who had his fingernails polished weekly? But he'd turned out to be the best thing ever to happen to his kid sister. But then he'd died, leaving Rina alone. She was too young to be a widow, but Jake found comfort in knowing she'd had happiness for a little while.

A union of opposites had worked well for Rina, but not for Jake. His marriage had ended in a bitter divorce because his wife hadn't realized that marrying a cop meant living on a cop's salary and adjusting to erratic hours. His wife hadn't just given up being married to a cop; she'd given up on Jake. And, after five years, it still hurt. Not because he still loved his wife but because he thought he'd given that kind of life his best shot. Still, Rina's marriage had flourished, and for that Jake was grateful.

"Money hasn't changed me." She sniffed, raising her chin in the air, pretending to take offense. "Well, not much, anyway. At least I walk him myself. I could pay someone to do it for me, but they'd quit after one day."

"High-maintenance breed?" Jake asked, watching the sexy waitress out of the corner of his eye.

"You could say that," Rina said.

He barely heard. *She* worked the inside restaurant, where the thickening crowd chose to sit. She impressed him with things that went beyond the superficial. Nothing fazed her—not the overwhelming heat, not the picky customer. She served with a thousand-watt smile, one he could watch all night. Especially since, every so often, she sent a covert look his way—to make sure he hadn't left? He liked to think so.

Because he sure as hell was aware of her. Jake couldn't recall the last time he'd been so sexually and emotionally conscious of a woman he didn't know. He hadn't been celibate since his marriage, but he hadn't gotten seriously involved, either. And none of the women in his far or recent past had piqued his interest in quite the same way *she* had. The sensual game they played intrigued him. He wasn't ready to end it by meeting her and destroying the fantasy. No woman could be as fresh and unjaded as she seemed to be. His marriage had taught him that.

Appearances, Jake knew now, were too often deceiving; women weren't always what they seemed. The sexy waitress attracted him more strongly than his ex ever had, and if that wasn't enough of a warning to steer clear, he had his current case to focus upon. He couldn't risk the distraction.

Rina waved a hand in front of his eyes and grinned. Obviously she knew his mind had been not on her words, but on the waitress who fascinated him. Considering he'd insisted on meeting at this place, at this hour, on the same night for the past few weeks, Jake figured his thoughts were pretty much transparent.

"As I was saying," she reminded him, "I had to walk Norton before meeting you, and he didn't want to go. I mean, he's trained to go on command, but you have to get him out onto the street, first. The poor thing hates the hot concrete on the pads of his paws. There I was, literally dragging him down Park Avenue, while he was trying to drag me back home. Can you imagine the sight?"

Jake shook his head. "The dog's a wuss," he muttered. He glanced over her shoulder, looking for the woman of his fantasies, but in the moment he'd refocused on Rina, *she* had disappeared. Disappointment gripped him as hard as the desire had earlier.

Rina patted his hand. "She'll be back. And Norton's not a wuss, he's just particular about what he likes, who he likes..."

"And who he doesn't," Jake said, recalling the puddle that had ruined his new sneakers on their first meeting.

"Well, regardless, he was Robert's dog, and I'm all he has left now."

Jake leaned forward in his seat. "So how are you, really?"

Rina had decided not to accompany her husband on a business trip, and he'd died in a car accident while rushing home to avoid an overnight stay. She'd been consumed with guilt and grief, and Jake had made it a priority to keep her spirits up. That included meeting her for dinner or drinks a few times a week. Almost a year had passed—a year in which Jake had kept up the routine because he enjoyed it, too. Rina was stronger now. Even the jokes had come more freely to her of late. Jake's mission had been a success. It had also recently led to his obsession with a woman he didn't know.

"Actually, that's what I wanted to talk to you about. How I'm doing. I'm going to take a vacation. A friend invited me to spend the summer with her in Italy. And I really need the break. I need to get away and…"

"I think it's a great idea." Jake didn't hesitate. Not only would the vacation do wonders for Rina's mental health, but it would keep her out of the country and safe until Ramirez was behind bars. "Anything that gets you out of that mausoleum of an apartment is good by me." Besides, all that marble and china made Jake nervous. Every time he turned around in the penthouse, he felt in danger of breaking something.

"I'm glad you think so. But about the penthouse?"

"Mausoleum."

"Whatever. I need you to stay there while I'm gone and watch Norton—and before you say no, think about the whirlpool and the pool. They'll do wonders for your rehabilitation.'' She opened her brown eyes wide and fluttered her thick lashes.

Not a good sign, he thought, and he knew he was in deep. ''I don't need physical therapy. I'm doing some exercises the orthopedist recommended, and my shoulder's just fine.'' He caught her stare and realized he'd been subconsciously rubbing the muscle with his hand. He quickly wrapped the hand around his glass, which had grown warm to the touch.

She raised an eyebrow. ''The department says otherwise.''

Much as he loved Rina, no way could he let her in on the fact that he had been undertaking strenuous rehabilitation. Her well-meaning concern often translated into talking at inopportune moments and generally butting into his life. He couldn't risk her informing the department that he'd be in shape sooner than they thought.

''The department has no say unless I choose to go back,'' he told her. And he was no longer sure he wanted to. Getting hit by a bullet and damaging his shoulder while diving out of harm's way had nothing to do with his uncertainty. The circumstances surrounding the episode did.

Louis Ramirez, who had been drug trafficking on college campuses and had access to major dealers, had been ripe for the picking. As a detective on narcotics detail, Jake had invested all his time and energy on the scum. He'd seen one too many co-eds in the morgue thanks to Ramirez's tainted goods, too many once fresh-faced kids now addicted. Jake had sworn he'd nail the crook, and had skirted the edges of proper police procedure to arrange a bust that would put Ramirez away for a long time. He'd trusted a snitch, something he regretted the instant the first bullet was fired and he realized he and his fellow officers had been set up.

But they'd gotten their man, anyway. After the hail of bullets that had stolen Frank's life and sidelined Jake, Ramirez had been taken into custody. And he would have stayed there, too, if Jake hadn't been down for the count. If some rookie hadn't screwed up and failed to give proper Miranda rights. Ramirez had walked, on a technicality. It wasn't the first time Jake had seen a criminal go free but it was the proverbial last straw. Jake was disgusted, disillusioned with his role in bringing in the dregs of the earth only to have his efforts thwarted courtesy of America's judicial system.

The detective Ramirez killed had been a good man—a man with a wife and kids—and though all cops knew the risk, Jake would have preferred to take the fatal bullet instead. *He* had no little ones who needed a father. Jake's weekend visits and phone calls to Frank's family were a poor substitute for the real thing.

"The system pisses me off and I've had it with the whole routine," he said, giving his sister the gut-honest truth.

"So Frank's gone and you're just going to give up?"

Her tone conveyed disbelief, possibly because she knew Jake better than anyone. She knew his friendship with Frank and his family ran deep and she understood the pain of losing someone. But she also knew her brother. Jake Lowell didn't throw in the towel, and he never left a job undone without a fight.

"I'll redirect my energies," he lied. He didn't want

to upset Rina by admitting he planned to get Frank's killer on his own.

Jake couldn't bring Ramirez in on any of the charges stemming from the original bust, but no doubt the guy was still selling drugs and somehow he'd slip up. Between Jake's off-duty digging and the official information two of his detective buddies continued to feed him, Jake would nab Ramirez. It was only a matter of time. But he wouldn't have the freedom to follow up leads if he was constrained by his superiors and newer cases he'd no doubt be assigned.

Jake also needed personal R-and-R. Time without the pressure and restrictions of the job to find out what direction he wanted to take in life. To decide what the restlessness he'd been experiencing lately meant. Was it the gritty life of a cop and the disillusionments that came with the job that had worn him down, or something more? Jake didn't have any answers. And he had a hunch none would be forthcoming until his mind was free of Ramirez.

His lieutenant would jump on him if he thought Jake was ready, so allowing a prolonged recuperation provided the perfect excuse. "Can we change the subject?" he asked his sister.

She shrugged. "Suit yourself. Let the muscle atrophy until you can't make it work. Then when you want to go back, you'll flunk the physical and—"

"Rina," he said, warning her with his tone.

But he understood her concern because it mirrored his feelings for her. There was nothing he wouldn't do for his sister. She knew it and played him shamelessly, but he adored her, anyway. Without a doubt, she had the same loyalty toward him, which prompted her pushing him now.

She held her hands up in surrender. "Okay, I'll back off. So will you stay in the penthouse while I'm gone?"

He raised an eyebrow. Given her usual propensity to butt in where she didn't belong, Jake didn't buy the easy subject change, but he was grateful for the reprieve. "Couldn't you put the dog in a kennel?"

"Norton doesn't like kennels. He gets nervous. And if you won't watch him, I'll have to stay home."

"Never mind," he muttered, resigning himself to animal- and apartment-sitting for the summer. His fate had been sealed from the moment she'd batted her brown eyes at him across the table. It didn't matter where he set himself up, as long as he had the freedom to come and go as he pleased on his quest for Ramirez.

With Rina out of town, Jake had nothing and no one cramping his movements. Besides, she needed the break. "You should get away, and if you need my help to do it, I'll stay, even if it means walking that pathetic excuse for a dog in public," he said, infusing his voice with warmth and humor. Once he said yes, he'd never knowingly make her feel guilty and, besides, he and Norton had developed a grudging respect for one another.

Her face lit up in a way Jake hadn't seen since before her husband passed away. "Oh, thank you."

Before he could blink, she was up and around the table. She wrapped one arm around his good side and kissed his cheek. "Thank you. You can't imagine how depressing it's been for me alone in the penthouse. This trip will help me put the memories behind me," she whispered.

"That's all I want for you." He squeezed her back.

"Now, can you get off me before the humidity glues us together?"

She laughed and resettled herself in the chair. "Now that we've dealt with my life, such as it is, it's time to deal with yours."

Jake groaned. "I knew my reprieve was too good to last. I'll make a deal with you. Go to Italy and have fun. Come back happy, and then we'll deal with my life." By then Jake should have Ramirez back behind bars where he belonged. But he knew Rina wasn't just referring to work.

Rina glanced over her shoulder. "I don't know, Jake. If you wait too long, someone might snatch her up. For all you know, she might already be attached."

"No ring," he said, and immediately regretted the admission.

"Then, do something about it," his sister said, challengingly.

He wanted to rise to the bait as he'd often done when they were children. But he couldn't. After his ex-wife, the only women he'd consider now were the ones who were safe, who didn't threaten his sanity or his heart. Considering the strong pull *she* exerted over him, Jake had a hunch this one was capable of doing that and more. With the Ramirez case hanging over his head, Jake didn't have time for distractions. And *she* was most definitely a distraction.

SHE WAS LATE. Brianne Nelson sprinted down the street toward The Sidewalk Café. She needed this second job and the money it brought in, but all she could think about was *him*. Was he here as he'd been last night and the night before that? Was he waiting or had he given up and gone home? And was he alone or, as usual, was he with the beautiful woman? The woman Brianne had seen hug him last evening.

Brianne's heart beat a furious pace, due more to anticipation and excitement than from her mad rush to make it to work. She'd thought she would never get out of the hospital. Her last client had gotten hung up in X-ray, and by the time Mr. Johnson arrived at physical therapy, he was forty-five minutes overdue for his appointment. After his second stroke, the older man needed rehabilitation as much as Brianne needed the money this waitressing job brought in. He had a new grandbaby he wanted to hold on his lap. She couldn't reschedule or hand him off to another therapist any more than she could give up her night job.

Nor did she want to. Not since she had the man of her dreams waiting. He arrived three times a week, wearing the same type of outfit—a pair of jeans and a shirt he'd obviously created himself with a pair of scissors and one good rip. The cropped shirt exposed a hint of tantalizing tanned skin, with a dark sprinkling of hair running down his abdomen until it disappeared into the denim waistband. And his forearms...she'd never seen muscles that well toned. He'd piqued her interest and fed her fantasies.

She slowed her pace as she reached the outdoor entrance, her gaze taking in the crowded tables on the sidewalk, lingering on the men seated outside. Though many had jet-black hair, none made her heart race. None met her gaze with a knowing gleam in his eyes or caused a liquid rush of desire in response to his sexy grin.

She shook off the disappointment caused by his absence, reminding herself that the man she anticipated was already taken. Meeting with the same woman *that* many times a week spoke of devotion and commitment—to someone else. Which was why she'd asked Jimmy to let Kellie handle the outdoor tables. Kellie was an accomplished flirt who rarely took any one man seriously, someone who could handle such a gorgeous customer with ease. Unlike Brianne, who had way too much interest in the man. Besides, even if he weren't involved, her dating and mating skills were rusty from disuse. Brianne understood her real life. *He* was a fantasy. She rushed in and past the bar.

"You're late," Jimmy called out.

"I'm sorry."

"Hang on. Someone wants to—"

She ducked into the small bathroom, cutting Jimmy off before he could lecture her about burnout again. He was her boss and in the process had become her friend. She was a physical therapist by day, and Jimmy understood how badly she needed this job at night. No matter how tired or how weary she was of smiling for the customers, she had no choice. She needed the money.

She was just fortunate Jimmy put up with her often delayed arrival; he rarely complained. Like her, he'd lost his parents young, and he'd also raised a sibling. He just hadn't had the added pressure of having a genius brother who deserved to remain in an exclusive, expensive, private boarding school and who would attend college thereafter.

Too bad her parents hadn't thought of either Marc or Brianne when they'd gone out in a small plane in weather that even the FAA had warned against flying in. Too bad they'd invested their money in pleasure and not in insurance for their children.

She shivered, then pushed all thoughts of her selfish,

risk-taking parents aside. She'd been her brother's only means of support for so long, she didn't know any different. But even a boss who was her friend couldn't keep her on if she didn't get her behind outside and start serving the customers.

Shoving her clothes under one arm, she paused to wash the grime of the New York City subway from her hands. Brianne wondered if *he* would show up later, and knew that thought would keep her going when her feet begged for a rest. Because, lately, she wasn't as tired, nor did she approach this job with the dread she had felt in the past. He kept her spirits high and her adrenaline flowing. Just knowing he'd be waiting, watching, making her feel sexy and desirable, when she had no time to *be* desirable, caused her anticipation to soar.

She air-dried her hands, then grabbed her clothes and turned toward the stalls. Before she could blink, she ran smack into a customer. "Sorry," she muttered.

"My fault."

Brianne took a step back and found herself face-to-face with the woman who usually sat with her fantasy man. Her dark hair was layered and razored in the most up-to-date style. The shaglike cut was perfect with her lightly made-up face and trendy clothes.

The woman certainly didn't look as if *she'd* spent the day massaging other people's body parts, Brianne thought, glancing down at her own scrubs. Then she looked at her watch and groaned before meeting the other woman's appraising gaze. "Excuse me. I'm running late." Brianne started for the open stall.

"Can we talk first?"

The other woman's voice stopped Brianne cold, and

she pivoted fast. "Excuse me?" Her heart beat more quickly.

They had nothing in common, nothing to discuss— except *him*. She'd done nothing wrong, Brianne assured herself. Yet the thoughts and fantasies she'd spun about a man she'd never met were enough to make her—a woman who'd seen men and women in varying degrees of nakedness during patient therapy— blush.

But no one she'd seen in patient therapy had even remotely resembled him. He was every inch a potent, sexy male who allowed her the freedom to feel like a woman, to test her limits and flirt without fear of anything more coming of it, because he was involved and she was too busy—which made him safe. Or so she thought.

"Hey, are you okay? I don't want you to faint on me," the woman said with concern.

Brianne nodded. "I'm fine," she said, embarrassment and shame filling her. Her fantasy man had a girlfriend who wanted to talk. Brianne had witnessed that hug between them last night with a pang of envy she hadn't known she was capable of feeling. But it served to remind her that he was spoken for. She cleared her throat. "I'm fine," she said again. "Thank you. It's just that I'm running very late. My boss…"

"Is a great guy. He said we could take a minute when you got in."

Brianne shook her head. "I'm not trying to be rude, but I really need to get to work. Jimmy's wonderful, but he can't compensate for the tips."

"I understand much more than you think. I come here often."

"I know." Brianne could have bitten her tongue for that admission.

"Yes, well, I don't want you to think I'm rude, or that I was eavesdropping, but..." She shrugged, and a sheepish grin lifted her lips. "I was eavesdropping. Last night. I heard you tell Jimmy how tired you were and how much you wished you could afford to get off your feet. And then he reminded you how much you want to move with your brother when he starts Stanford in the fall."

"And you'd like to put me on the first plane west?" Brianne asked with a hint of sarcasm.

"Yes. No." The woman let out a laugh. "I'd better just explain."

Brianne wasn't so sure she wanted to hear. If this woman thought Brianne was poaching on her boyfriend, she'd probably attempt to make California look good. Which it did—a new start for both her brother and herself. Physical therapy in a warmer climate, Brianne thought. Normal hours. Friends. A life.

She sighed. She'd sent résumés, but so far she hadn't had much luck. Either she'd been turned down flat or the salaries offered didn't come close to New York City's. Brianne had to be picky if she wanted to pay off Marc's boarding school loans and her own debts.

But reality aside, Brianne had a dream job in mind. A place she'd applied and still hadn't heard back from. If the Special Kid Ranch offered her placement, she hoped she could afford to take it. Working with children had always been her goal, one she hadn't been able to fulfill because the geriatrics job she'd gotten right out of school paid so well. Brianne didn't hold out much hope that the Ranch offer would come or be any better than those she'd had so far. She and Marc would be separated for the first time in both their lives—which was probably best for her brother's college experience, but still...

"Are you with me?"

Brianne blinked. "Yes. Sorry." She had so much on her mind these days, it was a wonder she functioned at all. Brianne refocused on the woman before her.

"I'd say we should sit and talk, but..." The other woman glanced around, taking in the tiled floor and single stall, and she grinned. "Well, you see the problem there. But just hear me out. I've got a proposition that I guarantee you won't be able to refuse."

# 2

BRIANNE STEPPED into the ornate lobby of the luxury building on the East Side of Manhattan. A uniformed doorman met her at the entrance and greeted her with a welcoming smile. "Hello, Miss Nelson."

Brianne paused, surprised the older man remembered her. She'd only met him once before, when she'd visited Rina earlier in the week. Brianne paused to take in the name on his badge before answering. "Hello, Harry." She smiled in return.

He tipped his head and ushered her toward the private elevator leading exclusively to the penthouse, then he punched the button and illuminated the up arrow.

While waiting, Brianne glanced around her. Glass and chrome gleamed brightly, showing off her reflection from every possible angle. She had to admit, the impact of the ornate lobby hadn't diminished on second viewing.

"You'll get used to it, miss."

The doorman's unexpected words told Brianne she looked as stunned as she felt. "I doubt it," she murmured. Not after living on bare necessities for so long. But she had no choice, seeing as how she'd be living here throughout the summer.

Without warning, the doors slid open. Brianne

stepped into the elevator and the doors shut quietly, leaving her alone with her disquieting thoughts.

She'd never believed she could be bought, but that was before the woman named Rina had made an offer Brianne couldn't resist. In return for being a physical therapist for Rina's brother in the evenings, Brianne would earn more than enough money finally to have a life of her own. She'd be able to pay off Marc's exclusive boarding school loans, and with his college costs covered by scholarships, her days of financial burden would be over. She'd even make a dent in her personal debt, thanks to the second part of Rina's offer—the back room in her penthouse, rent-free for the entire summer.

At the thought of moving in with Rina and her brother, virtually total strangers, Brianne's old anxieties threatened to resurface, but she battled them down with an ability she'd acquired over the years. Even if she hadn't met Rina's brother yet, Rina's warmth had been enough to put her at ease. There was no reason to fall back into old patterns created by her parents' dangerous and erratic lifestyle. Not now.

She had a larger concern—Rina's boyfriend. And Brianne hoped she wouldn't run into her sexy fantasy man during her time here. But Brianne felt certain that if Rina had an inkling of the attraction that had flowed between them, the other woman would keep them apart. Brianne swallowed at the painful notion, yet knew it was for the best—for Brianne, for her brother...for so many reasons.

The elevator cruised to a silent stop, and the doors slid open with a hushed glide. She stepped directly into the entryway and was overwhelmed by the large penthouse. Apparently Rina shared this place with her brother, an arrangement that would work well for Brianne's evening physical therapy sessions. Glancing around at the crystal chandelier above her, the wide expanse of windows and the marble floors, Brianne was struck again by the enormity of her quick decision. But as she'd told herself before, if a wealthy widow, as Rina had called herself, wanted to spend her money making her brother's life easier, Brianne would accept the residual good fortune and work hard in return.

She glanced down and smoothed the workout leggings she'd worn to meet Rina's brother. Instead of dressing to impress, she'd dressed down, intent to prove she wanted to work and was ready to begin. She wondered now if she'd made a mistake. Perhaps she should have opted for a better visual impression, but it was too late to change her mind. All that remained was the initial meeting with her new client.

*Difficult* was how Rina had described her brother. *Obstinate. Unwilling to continue therapy without being convinced.* Brianne covered her stomach with her hands, attempting to calm her nerves. She'd learned a long time ago how to cover her insecurities and make the most of any opportunity.

No time like the present, she thought. "Hello?" Brianne called into the empty apartment, surprised when she didn't hear an echo. The penthouse took up the entire top floor of the high-rise building, and no one could enter the private lobby elevator without the use of a passkey. She'd never been in any place as exclusive or as elegant as this. Or as empty, she thought. Considering the doorman had said she was expected, she wondered where Rina had disappeared to.

"Is anyone here?" she called out once more.

In response, the short, chubby dog she'd met on her last visit came bounding toward her, tail wagging in excitement and greeting. From his exuberance and glee, Brianne knew she had nothing to fear and bent down.

"Some watchdog you are." She had to dig beneath the wrinkles on his skin to give him a loving scratch behind his ears. "You're a cutey." She'd never seen a dog like this anywhere but on TV. She glanced at the dog tag beneath his neck for a reminder. "Is anyone else here, Norton?"

He licked her hand. "Black tongue," she murmured. "Interesting."

"Rina? What are you doing back?" A distinctly male voice called from somewhere inside the large apartment. Before Brianne could answer, he continued talking, his masculine voice coming closer. "I thought you were on your way to the airport. You didn't tell me the damn dog stands and licks your legs as you get out of the shower..." The voice stopped abruptly.

Brianne stood. She raised her gaze, and her breath caught in her throat. Her fantasy man stood before her—and he wasn't dressed. Unless she considered a couple of small towels, one around his waist and another around his shoulders, being dressed. She didn't, not when the parts that were uncovered were so muscular and spectacular. And he was tanned golden brown, except for the teasing glimpses of white skin below his waist, which disappeared beneath a towel that covered parts she didn't even want to think about.

Yes, she admitted, she did. She wanted to do more than think about them, and those illicit thoughts were rampaging as fast as her beating heart. Needing oxygen desperately, she tried to suck in a breath, then forced her gaze upward to meet his shocked stare.

"You're not Rina," he said.

Just as Brianne shook her head and wondered if he was disappointed, a sexy grin lifted his lips into the most unbelievable smile.

*Breathe,* she silently ordered.

"I didn't think you could be her. The limo picked her up for the airport a while ago."

Her eyes strayed to the towel riding low on his hips. She could handle this. She had to handle this. Her hands curled into tight fists. When she'd accepted Rina's proposition, she'd convinced herself she wouldn't be running into *him.* She was sure Rina wouldn't permit it. But she was seeing him here now.

And she'd be seeing a lot more of him, if he lived here, as she suspected he did. As if she wasn't seeing enough already. She watched in awe as the sun reflected off his tanned, muscular chest. Brianne grew dizzy and forced herself to inhale.

He took a step closer. The clean scent of soap mixed with a masculine spiced aftershave assaulted her, until she was enveloped in his essence. She couldn't take any more, not if she was going to maintain any dignity. "Don't move," she ordered. "Do not take another step."

"She speaks. And here I thought you were mute."

"Very funny," she muttered.

"Why can't I come closer?" He folded his arms low on his chest.

Damn, she wished he wouldn't do things that drew her attention to his body. Thanks to the many nights she'd spent fantasizing about him, her own body was on edge—her skin sensitized, her senses too aware of him. It didn't matter that they'd never actually met until now. This was a man she'd taken into her home, into her bed with her at night. And she now worked for the woman with whom he was involved. Brianne couldn't pretend the knowledge didn't bother her any more than she could pretend he didn't affect her.

Forget the money, there was no way she could take this job.

As if he could read her thoughts, Norton whined once, then placed his head down on the marble floor and looked up at her with soulful eyes. But when her fantasy man braced the knuckles of one hand beneath her chin and tipped her head upward so their eyes met and their gazes locked, she forgot all about the wrinkled dog.

His masculine fingertips were hot against her skin, branding where they touched. "You look like you're about to faint."

His body heat was potent. The urge to wrap herself around him and let his damp skin meld with hers was strong. Too strong. "I asked you not to come closer."

"And I asked you, why not? You never answered."

His eyes were a deep shade of blue, she realized for the first time, so dark they could be black, but with a hint of navy—or was it indigo?—giving them depth and interest.

She searched for a response that wouldn't leave her humiliated, and found none. She certainly couldn't tell him the truth. If he was a mind reader, she might as well jump off the roof of this very high, luxury building.

When she remained silent, he groaned and dropped his hand. "Okay, let's back up and try this again. I didn't know Rina was expecting company. Hell, I didn't know you and Rina even knew each other.''

Without his touch, she was able to focus a little more. ''We met last week. And Rina's not expecting me exactly, her brother is.''

He raised an eyebrow in definite surprise. ''He is?''

''I assume so. Rina said she'd let him know I'd be coming. I'm Brianne Nelson.'' Good manners dictated she extend her hand for a greeting. Self-preservation demanded she never touch him again. Considering he still stood in a towel and nothing more, Brianne figured she'd be forgiven for her lapse in social graces.

''Brianne,'' he murmured. Her name seemed to roll off his tongue. ''Beautiful. It suits you.''

''Thank you.''

He nodded. ''So tell me, why do you think Rina's brother is expecting you?''

Brianne narrowed her eyes. Wouldn't Rina have mentioned she'd hired someone as her brother's physical therapist? Or was their relationship so shallow, they didn't discuss anything of emotional importance? Somehow, she didn't think so. Brianne had sensed a depth to Rina, an innate sense of decency and caring. Much as Brianne would have enjoyed disliking the other woman, she just couldn't, which suddenly made this conversation even stranger than it already was.

She opted for minimal explanation. ''I'm a physical therapist.'' She didn't like the speculative gleam that came into his eye.

''I thought you were a waitress.''

Belatedly, she realized she knew no more about him than when she'd walked in, and she disliked being at a disadvantage. ''You know, this has become a very lopsided conversation. You know my name and occupations, but I know nothing about you."

"You know how I look fresh out of a shower," he said with a grin. "And that's an awful lot more than I know about you." He seared her with his deep eyes and a meaningful glance.

"That isn't what I meant."

He shook his head and laughed. "Sorry. Let's start over."

"We tried that already." She folded her arms across her chest—to cover her body's reaction to his heated stare and to ease the slow-building ache in her breasts.

"Then, let's do it till we get it right." He extended his hand.

In his eyes, she saw a definite challenge, as if he knew how much his touch affected her and dared her to grasp his hand, anyway. She had grown up with a younger brother and had learned to never back down from a dare. She steeled herself and placed her hand inside his.

"Jake Lowell," he said. "Nice to meet you, Brianne." He curled his large fingers around her smaller hand. Although she thought she'd been prepared, the connection between them was strong and sure—heated in a distinctly physical way and warm in a purely seductive one.

Without warning, his words registered; Rina had mentioned her brother's name. Brianne took a shocked step back. "*Jake Lowell?* You mean to tell me *you're* the one who needs therapy?" He grinned, and the air left her lungs in a rush. "*You're* Rina's brother?" she managed to ask.

"I'm Rina's brother, in the flesh." His grin grew wider.

Her gaze fell from his smile to the towel tucked in so that it looked about to fall open at the slightest provocation. She had no doubt that what lay beneath that towel was as incredible as the rest of him. She swallowed hard.

He wasn't Rina's boyfriend. He was Brianne's fantasy man. And she was his very own physical therapist, for as long as it took to both convince him to accept her help and bring him to full recovery. Fainting sounded good about now.

"And you're the surprise gift Rina said she'd leave for me while she was gone."

"Gone?" He'd mentioned something about a limo earlier, and Brianne's mouth grew dry.

"To Europe for the summer."

"You have got to be kidding."

He shook his head, looking more amused than she'd have liked. More of his earlier words came back to her. "You said she's gone and I'm the surprise gift?"

"Apparently so."

"What the hell do you mean I'm a gift?" Anger and betrayal oozed inside her, and seemed destined to grow. "Physical therapy isn't a gift; it's a necessity." And Rina had seemed to understand that.

She'd cared about her injured brother and wanted to speed his recovery despite his reticence, something Brianne could relate to. Her brother Marc had been a frail child, prone to illness and broken bones. Their parents hadn't appreciated having their extreme fun curtailed, and often had to hire a private physical therapist to rush his recovery.

Brianne had been fascinated by the seemingly magical healing powers the therapists had possessed, prompting her to follow in their footsteps. And though

Marc had eventually outgrown his childhood weaknesses, Brianne had never forgotten. Hence her desire to work with kids at the Special Kid Ranch, a place where she could heal children while they remained with their families.

*Family*. The word brought her back to Rina's ploy. Fury settled inside Brianne, and she felt as if she'd been punched in the stomach. She curled one arm around her waist for support. "Why in the world would she play this kind of game?" Brianne asked aloud, anger simmering.

"Oh, I can venture a guess."

He gestured back and forth between the two of them, and Brianne slapped her hand against her thigh and whirled around, starting for the door. Then she turned back again, not one to leave without letting her feelings be known. "Let me tell you something. I resent being taken advantage of. I take my job and my skills seriously. I'm not interested in some sort of matchmaking scheme." At least, that's what her mind insisted. Her rapidly beating heart begged to differ.

"Knowing Rina, it could very well be a scheme."

He stepped closer again, so close she felt his body heat.

"I wish you would stop doing that."

"How else can I prove you wrong?" His hand touched the pulse point in her throat, and she knew he felt it beating rapidly.

"Wrong about what?" she asked.

"You *are* interested." His voice dropped a seductive note.

"I'm about as interested as you are in need of therapy." She wondered briefly if he was involved in his sister's game, but his shock at seeing her here seemed so real, she dismissed the notion. She might not be able to blame him, but she was furious just the same.

"Then, I guess we have something in common." He reached for the corner of the towel hanging over his neck.

"What are you doing?"

"Making a point. See this?" Before she could argue or stop him, he lifted the towel high enough to reveal fading bruises across his powerful chest. "It was injured and my mobility's limited..." he lifted his arm, squinting as he moved, stopping obviously because of pain and an inability to go farther, "which means I am in need of physical therapy. So by your own admission, that means *you*, Brianne, are most definitely interested. In me."

She opened her mouth, then closed it again, her thoughts reeling, her heart pounding. He'd been injured, and she couldn't believe how knowing that affected her. She wanted to comfort him. To heal him. To make him all better.

She didn't want to pull her gaze from the faint bruising on his chest and shoulder, but dropped her eyes only to find herself focused on the towel barely covering his waist. Obviously he was serious, and Brianne forced her mind to the task at hand. She needed the money his sister had offered too much to walk away.

If she saw this job through to the end, she could afford to move west, even if she didn't get offered a job at the Ranch just yet. Working with Jake posed a challenge, but she'd never been a quitter, not even at the roughest, most exhausting points in her life. So what if she'd been manipulated into this job?

She pushed aside the hurt and anger and even managed to swallow some pride. *He* hadn't set her up; his sister had. But the benefits would be all hers in the long run, and that's all that mattered. She'd continue as planned, take this job, move into this apartment and rehabilitate this man's shoulder.

Oh Lord, what had she gotten herself into?

JAKE MET HER GAZE. Her eyes were wide, her lips parted. The desire to taste those lips had never been stronger. He didn't know what shocked him more— his sister's meddling or the woman she'd handpicked as her parting gift. Amazing that *she* turned out to be a physical therapist.

No matter what Brianne's occupation, Jake had no doubt Rina would have found a way to get them together. It just so happened that Brianne was the perfect woman to meet his current needs. And if she kept staring at the towel around his waist with blatant curiosity in her eyes, some of those needs were going to assert themselves, and soon.

He'd already gotten close enough to smell the lingering fragrance of strawberry in her hair. The scent was fresh and clean in a wholesome way, and yet it aroused a need so strong and intense, he'd been blindsided. For a man with a bad marriage and nasty divorce behind him, who stuck to low-maintenance, no-strings, unemotional relationships, his interest in this woman was too much.

He sure as hell hadn't expected to walk out and find her here. His only consolation was that she was obviously just as surprised and a whole lot shaken up. Jake understood. There was no denying the chemistry between them. But attraction was easy; what sizzled between them was not. Something more was at work here than lust. In her heavy-lidded gaze, Jake saw a depth of emotion that made the pull between them much more than just physical.

He had a hunch she sensed it, too, because in those eyes he'd also seen wariness. He'd thought Brianne—God, how he loved that name—would bolt given the chance. And he ought to let her, Jake thought. Having her here was a distraction he couldn't afford.

He needed his mind clear for the job at hand. Capturing Ramirez had to take precedence. He owed it to Frank and, more importantly, he owed it to Frank's family. Jake could barely face his buddy's wife and kids. Every time he answered to *Uncle* Jake, he felt like a goddamn fraud. He couldn't bring their father back, but he could make sure no one else lost someone they loved to a lowlife named Louis Ramirez. And he would do it himself, leaving no chance for someone else to screw up the bust again.

"Ready to discuss your rehabilitation, or do you intend to give me as hard a time as you've been giving your sister?" Brianne asked.

Her voice startled him back to reality. She seemed to shore up her defenses and her resolve. His sister had hired her to do a job, and from her squared shoulders and her determined expression it looked as if that's what she planned to do.

But rehabilitation was the last thing Jake wanted right now. Rina had obviously told Brianne that he'd been resisting rehab, and that was the impression he wanted the outside world to have. Brianne included. Everyone's safety—Frank's family's, Rina's, hell, even Jake's, hinged on taking Ramirez by surprise. Until Jake brought Ramirez in, he needed everyone to think he was being an obstinate SOB. And he could be, given the right motive, he thought wryly.

With Ramirez out of the picture, Jake could then decide whether or not he wanted to return to the force. He couldn't allow Brianne Nelson, physical therapist and the object of his desire, to threaten his "extended recovery." He couldn't have her reporting back to Rina with stories of his amazing improvement.

"You know what?" She cleared her throat. "Before we discuss anything more, would you mind putting on some clothes?"

A smile worked at his mouth. "If you insist." He'd been too floored seeing her here to give a thought to what he was, or wasn't, wearing.

"I have to insist."

He met her gaze and discovered that her eyes were a gorgeous shade of green that sparkled beneath the overhead, high-hat lighting.

"It would help establish the therapist-client relationship," she explained.

So she wanted to keep things professional. Or maybe she just wanted him to believe she did. It didn't matter either way. He knew as well as she did that nothing between them could ever be purely professional. Around her, his heart beat harder, his adrenaline flowed faster, and he was more interested in her than he'd been in anything other than Ramirez since the shooting. He needed the distance she was attempting to place between them too badly to allow their sizzling attraction to screw up his head or his case— something he figured could happen very easily. As long as she wanted to hide behind the illusion of safety, Jake would let her.

Norton had settled himself on the floor at her feet.

Obviously the dog was smarter than Jake had given him credit for. "I'll take him with me. Come on, boy."

Norton lifted his head, then placed it back down between his front paws. Jake groaned. He'd spent the better part of the morning trying to coax the dog out of the moping depression he'd fallen into when Rina had left, suitcases in hand. All he'd gotten for his effort was the doggie bath on his legs when he'd gotten out of the shower. Other than that, the mutt sat crying by Rina's bedroom door. He glanced from the dog lying happily at Brianne's feet, to her beautiful face.

He had to admit Norton had taste. And at least that pathetic whining had stopped. "Do you mind if he stays with you?" he asked, wishing he could do the same thing but knowing he needed some time alone to figure out the best way to avoid rehabilitation with his newly hired therapist.

She knelt and patted the dog's head. "Of course, I don't mind. We've become friends, haven't we, boy." With a prolonged sigh, Norton rolled onto his back, giving her access to his stomach and other body parts Jake would prefer not to see.

He rolled his eyes. "Kiss-ass," he muttered, then turned to Brianne. "Make yourself at home." He gestured to the living room and hoped she didn't mind the velvet couches or the marble statues. They weren't him, but they were here, and there was nothing much he could do about it except get through the summer.

"Thanks," she murmured.

Jake turned and headed for the master bedroom Rina had insisted he take as his own. His body burned and sizzled, and he knew without turning back that Brianne's gaze followed his retreat. He changed into clothes, still having no idea how best to avoid her rehab.

Then the telephone rang. He grabbed the receiver. "Hello?"

"Jake?"

It was Rina. If she hadn't already sounded out of breath, Jake would have liked to strangle the breath out of her.

"Listen, I have some seating problems and I need to rush, but I wanted to check. Did—?"

"Brianne's here," he muttered. "And you should have butted out, Rina."

"You and I spent enough time at the café for me to know better. Fate doesn't send many gifts, and when one arrives, you can't turn it away. The time Robert and I shared was too short. I want more for you. All I did was give you that chance. You can't be mad at me for pumping her boss for a little information. She was heaven sent, Jake. You *need* her."

In frustration, he ran a hand through his hair. If he wondered why he'd kept his rehab from Rina, she'd just reminded him. Any time she decided she knew what was best, there was no stopping her. Thank God she was headed for Europe. He couldn't risk her messing with his career next.

He shook his head. "Isn't it up to me to decide who and what I need?"

"Oh, did you hear that? They're paging me. Maybe they found someone to switch seats. You know I can't stand the window. I get claustrophobic, not to mention that I can't get up and pee as often as I like on such a long flight."

He rolled his eyes.

"Oh, and Jake? Before I go, did I mention Brianne

will be moving into the spare room off the back hall? She was able to break her lease, and it's so much more convenient for your workouts. Besides, I know she needs…'' The rest of his sister's sentence was cut off by a loud voice over a sound system. ''I'm sorry, Jake. I really have to run. I'll call from Italy. I love you.'' And then she was gone, leaving Jake dizzy from her rushed admission.

And he damn well was concerned by her information. He lowered himself onto the bed, trying to absorb his sister's news. His solitary existence was about to be royally screwed up. He'd no sooner gotten Rina safely out of the country than he had another female on his hands. At least this one wasn't a relative. She had no overt ties to Jake, which made her safe from any retaliation by Ramirez. The thought brought him marginal comfort.

He couldn't completely relax because he still had Brianne and their sizzling attraction to deal with. She was right in thinking they'd been set up. And he was right in thinking the physical therapy angle had made Rina's matchmaking easier. But Rina would have found a way to move her in here even if Brianne had been a taxi driver.

Brianne had broken her lease and given up her apartment. She'd obviously accepted this job in good faith and was here to stay. There wasn't a thing Jake could do about it. He couldn't fire her or throw her out on the street. But no matter how much he desired her—and even now his body throbbed with yearning—she definitely didn't fit into his summer plans. Her presence would put his ability to come and go as he pleased at risk, compromising his freedom and private agenda to nab Ramirez.

Once she moved in here, with him… The realization sunk in, slamming into his gut with startling clarity. The woman he'd desired for months was about to become his roommate. Not even a cold shower could douse the heat that thought inspired. He'd spent too many nights, after leaving the café, tossing and turning in his bed, thinking of her, yearning for the touch of a woman who existed only in his fantasies. Yet those fantasies were real enough for his sheets to rasp against his naked, aroused body. Real enough for his hands to become her hands, and for him to be spent, but not satisfied, thereafter.

But things were different now. Because, this time, she was more than a face, more than a fantasy. She had a name and a personality. Like it or not, she was his very own physical therapist who was moving in with him for the duration of the summer.

And she was waiting for him in the other room.

# 3

BRIANNE WALKED to the array of windows that offered a perfect view of the East River. Norton followed, his dog tags jingling behind her.

The sun's rays were strong through the thick glass, heating her skin as well as the room. Not that she needed any more body heat. There wasn't a part of her that wasn't already on fire, thanks to Jake. A sexy name for a sexy man. A sexy, single and unattached man, she thought, again taking in the marble floors, sculpted works of art and modern paintings adorning the walls in the apartment he shared with his sister. From the mundane to the more in-depth aspects of his personality, there was a lot she didn't know about Jake Lowell. She wondered what he did for a living, even what he liked to eat for breakfast.

Basically, she questioned everything about him, but she decided here and now, she wouldn't ask. She couldn't afford to find out. Jake excited her, but she'd have to keep their relationship professional. It wouldn't be easy. This man, this apartment, this chemistry between them—all were the stuff from which fantasies were made. But fantasies didn't come true; she knew that firsthand.

She'd wanted loving, concerned parents, and she'd gotten world travelers, more interested in their dangerous adventures than their children. She'd wanted security and the opportunity to live a normal life. To go out when her friends did, to date and to have fun. Instead she'd gotten the responsibility of a brother she loved more than life itself and the emotional and financial burden of seeing to it that he was raised right. More than most people, Brianne understood fantasies were necessary to ease life's burdens, but they never came true.

Her aching desire for the man in the other room would remain in the realm of impossible dreams. It had no place in her real life. The less she learned about Jake Lowell, the safer she would be. As it was, taking this job would be hazardous to her mind, her heart and, most definitely, her body. How she would live here with him and survive the summer, she had no idea.

Physical therapy itself was extremely hands-on. Her palms would cover his upper back and shoulders, and ease around to the front of his chest. Her fingers would massage his strong muscles. She'd be getting up-close and personal with a man who sent her senses soaring and who'd unexpectedly touched her emotions as well. Brianne saw scars and injuries every day of her life, yet when she'd looked at Jake's, an aching tenderness had risen to her throat. She didn't know why he affected her so, but she knew it didn't bode well for her vow to remain detached, to be the professional she was being paid to be.

But she would if it killed her.

"I'm ready." His deep voice sent tremors of awareness racing through her.

He might be ready but she wasn't. Brianne turned to face him. She could have handled it if he'd dressed in a Polo collared shirt and starched khaki pants. That would have created distance. Instead he wore his standard ripped sweatshirt, this one in navy, which brought out the depth of color in his eyes, and a pair of sweat shorts that didn't come much lower than the towel had earlier.

At the sight of him, her heart began a steady, rhythmic beat. She sighed. Time to get things between them settled. "You're ready. How interesting. Rina led me to believe you'd be a difficult patient. In fact, she said you'd be a hard sell. That you'd resist therapy."

He shrugged. "And Rina was right. I meant I'm ready to talk." He stepped over to the couch in the living room and seated himself on a velvet sofa. With his day's growth of beard and his casual clothes, he appeared ridiculously out of place in the formal room, and yet nothing could detract from his rugged, bad-boy good looks.

"Join me." He patted the space beside him.

Knowing she had no choice if she wanted to persuade him, she walked over and lowered herself onto the soft cushion, not as close as he'd suggested. But his masculinity couldn't be denied, and even with a good amount of distance separating them, Brianne felt his powerful presence. *Think professional,* she reminded herself. And when her gaze fell to the enticing skin between the ragged edge of his shirt and the waistband of his sweats, Brianne again reminded herself to breathe.

"Tell me something, Jake."

"Say that again."

She tipped her head to the side. "What?"

"My name."

He leaned forward until he was too close. His breath

held a refreshing hint of mint, and her stomach curled with a delicious warmth.

"Jake," he said. "Say it again."

His gaze locked with hers and held. She couldn't have turned away if she wanted to, and, heaven help her, she didn't want to. Because she understood. They'd spent the past couple of weeks in silken, seductive silence. Her name on his lips had sounded so very sweet. She couldn't deny him the same pleasure.

"Jake," she murmured.

His eyes glazed and he inched closer, kissing distance away. The tingling scent of mint surrounded her, tempting her, teasing her.

"I've been curious for so long."

His masculine voice reached deep inside her, and she couldn't lie. "Me, too." And curiosity was the only reason she'd allow the inevitable kiss, or so she told herself.

He touched her beneath her chin, holding her head in place as his mouth settled over hers. Strong and sure, yet achingly gentle, his kiss was everything she'd dreamed about, yearned for. And when his searching tongue traced her lips, moistening before slipping inside, her entire body shook in reaction. Pulsing began in her chest and settled lower, between her legs, strengthening the desire that had built between them from across a crowded room.

His breath was warm and minty, his mouth hot and needy, just as she was, and a sigh of pure pleasure escaped her throat. He caught her sigh in his mouth and used it as permission to deepen the kiss. But the sound she'd made shook her out of the haze of desire and back into reality. *Therapist and client,* she reminded herself, and forced her hands to his shoulders—not to feel the firm muscles beneath the sweat-shirt, but to push him away.

Unfortunately, the motion took longer than she'd planned, as she first curled her fingers around the soft cotton and his flesh beneath. She allowed the pro-longed kiss to go on for another sweet minute before breaking contact.

Shaking off the temporary insanity that had over-come her wasn't as easy. "We can't do this."

He swallowed, his throat moving up and down be-fore her eyes, his breathing as ragged as hers. "Can't do what? Get acquainted?"

She licked at her damp lips, his lingering taste fu-eling the desire still flickering inside her. "That was more than getting acquainted." Then the rest of his words registered. "Are you saying you've changed your mind about rehab?"

He shook his head and laughed. "I like your strat-egy. Kiss me and lower my defenses. Are you trying to take advantage of me?" A smile tipped the corner of his mouth.

"You kissed me first," she reminded him.

"You didn't stop me."

They sounded like squabbling children, but there had been nothing juvenile about that kiss. "Let's just say we got it out of our systems. Now we can move forward."

"And you can move in?" He shrugged with his one good shoulder. "That was Rina on the phone. She just explained the new living arrangements." His gaze in-tense and curious, never left hers, as if he were trying to read her thoughts.

But she couldn't deny that he looked surprised by his sister's call and revelation. As surprised as he'd appeared when he'd discovered her in the apartment earlier. "Obviously you didn't know about that, either?" she asked.

He shook his head. "No."

"I think this is called manipulation," she muttered.

"Blatant," he agreed. "But that's Rina. Always with the best intentions, but not always thinking up here." He tapped the side of his head. "She's a romantic."

"It's nice to see people still are." Her own heart pounded frantically in her chest, their kiss still lingering in her mind.

"My parents are one example. Retired, living in Florida and driving each other crazy. Rina's another. She's the secretary who married her wealthy boss. In her eyes, all things are possible."

She wondered what things were possible in his. Did her fantasy man who kissed like a dream also harbor a belief in fairy tale endings? She shook her head, knowing her deluded thoughts and curiosity could only get her in trouble. "Does Rina's romanticism extend to getting her stubborn brother into physical therapy by moving me in here?"

"I guess so." He grinned a charming I'm-cute-and-I-know-it grin.

She'd already accepted the setup before that mind-blowing kiss. She couldn't back down now, and her reasons were the same. She needed the money from this job to start her life over. She needed to move in, rehabilitate Jake's shoulder and put her desire for him behind her.

Brianne glanced down. Norton lay at her feet, looking up at her with adoring eyes. Two cute males in one large apartment. However would she survive it?

One way was to get things between them out in the open. "Okay, Jake. Tell me exactly where we stand on the subject of physical therapy. Obviously you're resistant, you've given your sister a hard time over the subject…"

"Of course I have. Do you have a brother or sister?"

She nodded. "A brother."

"Then, you know siblings live to give each other a hard time."

No, Brianne didn't know. Because she'd been more of a parent to Marc than a sister, she'd never experienced classic sibling rivalry. She'd been too busy waitressing while finishing school and taking care of Marc at the same time to indulge in normal family dynamics. "Marc's a good deal younger than me. Our relationship was—is different. But I'm not here to talk about my brother. Rina hired me for a reason, and I want to know if you're going to let me do my job or not. I want to know what to expect from you."

Jake forced a lighthearted smile. He had no idea what to expect from himself. That kiss had caught him off guard. He hadn't planned to be so forward, and sure as hell hadn't expected her to kiss him back. Or to taste better than he'd dreamed.

If he'd wondered how much trouble she could cause him, he now knew. "If Rina hired you, I certainly can't throw you out."

"Gee, thanks," she said wryly. "But the question is, will you cooperate?"

The professional was back. Jake told himself he was glad, but deep inside he knew he lied. He liked the warmer, softer Brianne better. Still, this one was safer.

And he had to play it safe, too, keep it light, and

keep her off guard. That way she wouldn't get too close or discover he was further along in rehab than she and Rina believed. "I'm sure I can be persuaded. And I'm certain you're up to the task."

"So all of a sudden you're willing to consider therapy?"

He shook his head, seeking to buy time. "I'm willing to let you try and persuade me."

"Why the turnaround?"

"No turnaround. I haven't agreed to anything yet."

She raised an eyebrow, obviously unsure what to make of him. "But you will."

"That certain of yourself and your abilities?"

"Absolutely. The only question I have is, why the change?"

She'd read him well, Jake thought. Or rather, she read *them* well. Did she really have to ask why he'd end up working with her despite his token resistance? "Do you want me to tell you the truth? Or what you want to hear?"

Jake had the distinct impression that the answer was "both." She wanted to know the only reason he'd even consider rehabilitation was to get close to her. And she wanted him to lie so she didn't have to face it.

"I'll consider therapy because of you."

She exhaled hard.

"Just like you're not going to walk out on this job because of me." He grinned.

"You're a cocky one," she murmured with a smile.

"And this is a good thing?"

"Sure is. It means you can take a tough workout." She met his gaze head-on.

She hadn't backed off at his admission. Even after

that kiss, she wasn't intimidated by the attraction between them. Score one for her, Jake thought. He admired her grit—something he rarely found in a woman.

It also helped his cause. She'd need that strength if they were going to bump into one another in the middle of the night, stealing a drink from the fridge. *He* would need that strength. "I can take anything you dish out, sweetheart. Just tell me what you have in mind."

"You might be sorry you asked. Physical therapy involves strengthening with rubber bands and working the muscle with massage therapy." The word *massage* hovered in the air between them and the blood pulsed inside him, making him ache as if her hands were already on his body.

"But water therapy works well, too," she continued. "The resistance in the water is a help. Add a whirlpool, and the pulsating water jets work wonders to loosen the muscle," she said, her voice resonating with a deep, husky quality.

"Pulsating water jets, huh?"

Her face flushed red. "Different therapists take different approaches, but there are many options."

He wondered if she was imagining them naked in the whirlpool, water flowing freely around them. He wondered if she had any idea what fun two people could have in that whirlpool she'd mentioned, water jets and all. "It all sounds interesting, especially the pulsating water jets." He wiggled his eyebrows provocatively.

"I'll just bet." Watching him warily, she folded her arms over her chest and studied him. "I save the water therapy for my most cooperative patients," she said in a provocative, seductive voice.

Just as she probably had intended, his body began a steady rhythm, one that only those vibrating water jets could match. He sucked in a breath and forced himself to think like the cop he still was. First and foremost, he needed information about her schedule, if only so he could better plan his. When would she be in the penthouse? When would he be on his own? When could he slip out to work on the Ramirez case without her reporting back to his sister?

"So, when do you start—convincing me, I mean? Because with the right incentive, I can be *very* cooperative." And damn if he didn't want to comply with any and all of her water-related directives. "I'm a quick learner—and an even better instructor."

He watched her struggle to maintain her composure. He was glad. If he kept her off balance, he'd be more in control. He needed that control, since he could too easily dismiss Frank and his family, and Ramirez in favor of Brianne. It disturbed him to realize that despite her ability to screw up all he'd worked for, he wanted her.

She cleared her throat. "Relax, water boy. We start as soon as I get a referral, diagnosis and prescription from your doctor. Probably sometime next week."

He glanced at Brianne. She'd leaned against the couch, still professional but more relaxed, so certain she'd bought herself time before having to deal with him and his reluctance to begin therapy. Before having to convince him the only way he'd allow—a seductive, playful coaxing. Because as long as Brianne would live and work here, Jake intended to control the situation.

He ignored the voice in his head reminding him that he'd been seconds away from relinquishing control and turning the kiss from sensual to sinful, from easing her onto the couch and satisfying the basic yearning he'd had since laying eyes on the sexy waitress. Neither would or could happen, of course, or she'd know exactly how in shape his shoulder was. The games he'd coax her into playing as she attempted to seduce him into therapy would have to suffice.

She obviously recognized his intent and hoped for some breathing room that would come with waiting for the doctor's response. Too bad for her peace of mind; the paperwork was in the other room. He'd had it for weeks. He just hadn't used it because a close friend had been helping him privately. "Sorry, but you don't get that kind of space, hon."

"Don't call me that."

"Does it offend you?" he asked.

She shook her head. "No, it turns me on."

Jake turned wide eyes her way.

She let out a laugh. "Sorry. I just can't let you think you'll always have the upper hand."

He inhaled slow and deep, forcing himself *not* to concentrate on what she had just said. Not to contemplate the possibilities of her actually being aroused. Right now. By him. "I have the referral and paperwork in the other room," he told her.

As he'd expected, that dimmed the wattage on her smile. "I need to get myself settled."

"How long?"

"Not very," she admitted. "Rina's offer was so amazing, I spent last week organizing."

"Can I help you move your things?"

Her gaze fell to his shoulder. "If you can manage that, you don't need me."

She was dead wrong. He definitely needed her. He just couldn't afford to. "I'm certain you have some kind of use for me."

She laughed. "I'm not going to touch that one."

The sound settled inside him, making him feel more alive than he had since he'd both lost his best friend and injured his shoulder.

"Jimmy—you know, the owner of the café—can help me move in."

Jake nodded, ignoring the unwelcome and unfamiliar stab of jealousy he felt at hearing another man's name on her lips. He changed the subject to one more interesting. "I suppose Rina mentioned there's a private gym, a pool on the roof, as well as that whirlpool?" he asked.

"The subject came up, yes. Although if you'd like to look into doing therapy at the hospital, we could use the facilities there."

"I was referring to you using the pool and whirlpool in your free time. Not for therapy."

"Oh, that's right. You haven't agreed to anything yet."

He grinned. "Exactly right."

She rolled her eyes. "Care to tell me why not?"

He averted his gaze.

"Guess not."

He wondered if he imagined the disappointment that flashed across her features when he didn't confide in her, and refused to dwell on why her feelings bothered him. "I'm curious. What exactly was the deal you made with Rina?"

She shrugged as if the answer were basic. "Private physical therapy."

"When, Brianne?" He drew out her name, liking the feel of it on his lips. "How often?" He figured Rina would have pinned her down for two to three days a week, and told himself he needed to know the schedule she expected him to follow should he agree to therapy. But a part of Jake wanted to hear that she'd committed to more.

"I work rehab at the hospital during the day, so your therapy would be in the evenings."

His evenings lately had been routine—dinner, television and bed—and he suddenly envisioned a wealth of sensual opportunities with a woman who interested his mind as well as his body, then mentally decked himself because he needed his nights free in case he got a tip on Ramirez. "How many nights a week?"

"At least five."

He forced a laugh. "Rina's a slave driver. I'm sure we can work out something easier on you. After all, you work days, too."

She shook her head. "I made a deal and I'll work what I'm being paid for." Her green eyes zeroed in on his. "You're not getting off that easily."

Knowing what was good for him, Jake took her warning seriously.

BRIANNE HAD BEEN GIVEN a reprieve. She couldn't move into the penthouse until she'd packed up her things and she couldn't start working on Jake until she satisfied her obligation to Jimmy. She wouldn't desert her current employer without fair notice.

She'd bolted from the penthouse last night because she'd needed space—fresh air that didn't include

Jake's seductive, masculine scent. If she hadn't gotten out of that apartment, she might have succumbed to his easy grin and seductive charm. She might have been tempted to steal another kiss.

She had a hunch he wouldn't have stopped her. And she wouldn't have been satisfied with just one.

She curled up on her bed, the morning light spilling through the window, and pulled out the paperwork Jake had given her earlier. Many of the answers she didn't want to know lay before her. If she read these papers, she'd be given insight into him as a man. He would become more real, more flesh and blood than he was to her already.

But she didn't have a choice. She hadn't wanted to think about the fact that she'd have to look into his medical records and background before being able to begin physical therapy. That decision had been made, however, so Brianne took a deep breath and unfolded the documents.

One glimpse and her head spun in shock, disappointment and concern. He was a cop, a detective, injured on the job, who needed rehabilitation in order to return to active duty. By providing the physical therapy, she'd be giving him back his career, and enabling him to put himself in danger again.

Apparently she was destined to have her life filled with risk-takers, people whose adrenaline only flowed when in the midst of excitement. She sighed. Well, at least now she had a concrete reason to not let herself get involved with Jake on any level other than the professional.

As if the probability of her leaving for California at the end of the summer wasn't enough of a deterrent to beginning any kind of relationship with this sexy, compelling man, she now had his hazardous occupation. She'd lost her parents and lived through the aftermath of their risk-taking. She'd built her present, established a future and gotten a handle on the way she wanted to live. No way she'd let herself lose her heart or her peace of mind that way ever again. Even if the man excited her in ways she desperately wanted to explore.

Leaving the papers on the bed, she headed for the shower. Anything to soothe her. She stripped off her clothes, turned on the water and stepped inside. Hot water on the hardest massage setting pelted her already sensitized skin. Kissing Jake had aroused her, and now she needed the stinging sensation against her flesh to dull the need he'd inspired.

But as the steady stream of water drilled her skin, instead of dulling the ache, it fanned the flame of desire. Her breasts felt heavy, her nipples tight and the sensitive flesh between her legs full to bursting. She tried to tell herself that the way her blood raced through her veins was a response to the knowledge of freedom. That she was reacting to the lure of having a life.

When the summer was over and her time with Jake complete, she'd move west and start over. She could just work one job and have the liberty to come home after work and curl up with a book, or to date a man instead of working a second shift. But Brianne knew she was deceiving herself about the reason for her excited state.

She was responding to Jake, to his flirtatious manner and the sizzling sexual awareness that shimmered between them. But it was an awareness that could go nowhere. She flipped off the water, knowing the shower was doing nothing to dampen her aroused state. No man had ever affected her so strongly, and nothing could ease the building desire.

She stepped out and grabbed for the fluffy towel she'd left hanging behind the door. Steam filled the bathroom, making her hotter than she'd been minutes earlier, if that were possible. Lifting her foot to the edge of the tub, she patted her leg dry, moving upward to her thigh. And she thought about Jake's injury and the bruising that discolored the otherwise perfect, tanned flesh. She thought about his pain and wanted to ease it.

And she would. With caressing brushes of her fingertips and with stroking movements across his skin. But what would stop her from moving lower? From easing her hands from his shoulder to his hair-roughened chest, to the puckered, darkened nipples just begging for her touch?

What would prevent her from then dipping lower, tracing his firm abdomen, and passing the waistband of his shorts until she encountered the other powerful muscle that would be rigid and firm, waiting for her?

And what would stop him from reciprocating? From moving his strong hands between her legs, from slipping his fingers between the folds of her flesh and easing the ache with slow but sure thrusts? What would stop him from picking up her personal rhythm and from making slow and sure become quick and fulfilling?

Absolutely nothing. The answer came to her immediately, and Brianne's breath flowed in shallow gasps as she realized her own hands mimicked her desire, arousing her wanting flesh. And she realized nothing could stop what was about to happen. Meeting him had fanned the flame that had been lit at the moment of their first illicit glance. His sexy voice and seductive touch had sent her over the edge.

Nothing could stop the fantasy.

Nothing could stop them.

Bright light and a wash of pleasure, strong and enveloping, rushed through her. And Jake's name was on her lips.

AFTER A LONG DAY at the hospital, Brianne headed over to the restaurant to say goodbye to Jimmy one last time. She'd promised him two weeks' notice, but when she'd arrived and given him details, he'd practically fired her on the spot. Jimmy knew how much money was at stake and refused to let her risk losing the opportunity. More than most, Jimmy understood the freedom Rina's payment would provide.

Brianne packed the small stash of things she kept at The Sidewalk Café, a duffel bag with feminine and emergency items, then zipped it closed. "I'm set. I hate to leave you shorthanded, though," she said, turning to Jimmy.

He leaned both elbows on the bar. "Sweetheart, much as I love you, there's no shortage of waitresses in New York City."

"Are you saying you won't even miss me when I'm gone?" She placed her hand over her heart and feigned a heavy sigh.

"You're dedicated and loyal—but rarely on time, and you took ages and three sets of dishes to train. Remind me again why I kept you on?" He winked, and a lock of sandy-blond hair fell over his forehead.

"Oh, you." She tossed a wet rag his way. "It wasn't that bad."

"Speak for yourself." His mouth tipped upward in a grin, showing dimples that charmed many women and brought in a harem most weekend nights.

Brianne was grateful for his friendship and support, but he hadn't appealed to her that way—not the way Jake had. And though Jimmy had asked her out, he'd always respected the boundaries of friendship and accepted her no's after the first couple of easy letdowns. With all they had in common, he'd become her closest friend and her brother's male role model when he was home from boarding school.

"Seriously, though, if this guy puts any moves on you, you give me a call."

Brianne stifled a cough, knowing any *moves* Jake made wouldn't be unwanted, just unwise. "Thanks, but I'll be fine." She slung her bag over her shoulder, refusing to let even Jimmy see her bad case of nerves over taking this new job. "And you lay off the cigarettes, okay? They'll kill you if some woman doesn't do it first," she said with a grin.

He shook his head and laughed. "I'll be at your place bright and early to help you move in." He ignored the cigarette reference, just as she'd expected.

"You're a prince, Jimmy."

"That's what they all say. You aren't angry at me for setting this up, are you?"

"How can I be angry when you dug me out of a deep hole? I finally see daylight. I'm grateful, even if you do have a big mouth." She grinned, letting him know she was joking. Gossip was a hazard of his bartending occupation. She couldn't fault him.

"You'll keep in touch?"

She nodded. "You bet. Tell Kellie I'll call." She had a hunch after one night in the penthouse with Jake, she'd be needing both Jimmy and Kellie's differing gender advice. She also had her friends at the hospital, especially Sharon, another physical therapist in whom she could confide. But there was something about Jake she wanted to keep close and private, share with as few people as possible, Brianne thought.

"Take care, Bri."

She walked around the bar and gave her best friend a hug, then she strode out into the humid evening air. Heat wafted upward from the sidewalk, but Brianne had a feeling her nights were about to get even hotter.

THE PRECINCT smelled familiar, Jake realized as he walked into the place. Musty and old with linoleum floors and chipped-paint walls, it had been the place he'd called home for many years. He'd joined the force straight out of state college and never looked back. Until now.

Nodding as he passed people in the hall, Jake entered the squad room and pulled up a chair by a metal desk. "Hey, Duke."

"Jake, buddy, how are you doing?" Duke Russell, his good friend and fellow detective, slid his chair back and stood, clapping him on the back.

Jake swallowed hard and refrained from wincing. "Hanging in." He settled himself into a nearby chair. "Any news on Ramirez?" Duke and Steve Vickers were feeding Jake information.

"We can keep this between us?"

"Haven't we always?"

Duke nodded his head. "Nothing's changed. Like I've been telling you, Ramirez walked out of the courtroom and, from all reports, he's living a clean—albeit sleazy—life. Not that we've stopped keeping tabs on him.''

"Well, damn." Jake reached over and grabbed a box of TicTacs from the corner of Duke's desk, shaking one into his hand and popping it into his mouth. The fresh peppermint cleared his palate but not the residual sour taste from a case gone bad. He leaned forward and spoke low. "Ramirez can't stay clean forever. His girlfriend claims she hasn't seen him."

"You're on injury leave, and I told you Vickers would take care of that shit on patrol. You're supposed to be coordinating from home. What the hell are you doing talking to Ramirez's girlfriend? The lieutenant will have your ass if he finds out."

Jake shrugged. "What the hell's he going to do? Throw me off the force?" Jake didn't know if he wanted to be there, anyway. He only knew he wasn't leaving this case open, and as long as Ramirez was walking the street, free to peddle drugs to kids and take down good men, the case remained unsettled.

"Lowell!" The barking voice reverberated through the room. That bark had intimidated more junior officers than Jake had fingers on both hands, but he'd never let the lieutenant mess with his head. As a result, a grudging respect had developed over the years. Lieutenant Thompson didn't appreciate Jake's often renegade style, but as long as Jake didn't cross the line, the lieutenant gave him leeway. Each respected the other's boundaries.

But this injury had tested both men. Thompson wanted his detective back; Jake wanted to take his time, first on Ramirez and then on deciding what the hell life had in store. Opposing goals with no middle ground.

Until Brianne, Jake thought, realization dawning. He'd thought having her around would cause nothing but problems, but she'd just given Jake a means of keeping Thompson happy and buying himself time. He hadn't told the lieutenant he'd been in therapy before because Thompson knew his therapist Alfonse, and Alfonse couldn't lie worth a damn if questioned. But if anyone talked with Brianne, she'd tell the truth— Jake was being a pain in the ass and she was working on him slowly.

Jake rose from his seat and turned. "Afternoon, Lieutenant."

"I thought I told you I didn't want to see your sorry ass in here unless you were in rehab."

Jake inclined his head. "Never say I don't follow orders, Lieutenant."

The older man snorted. "That'll be the day."

"No kidding. I've got myself my very own physical therapist. It'll just take a while till I'm up to speed," he said.

Thompson narrowed his eyes, his suspicion evident. "I won't ask what changed your mind."

"Good, because I wouldn't tell you."

Thompson turned his steely gaze toward Duke. "You'd better not be spilling department secrets."

Duke shook his head. "It's not like he's an outsider."

"He damn well is. At least until he aces his physical and gets his ass back in here."

Jake laughed. "I think this is what they call talking about me like I'm not in the room."

"Shut the hell up, Lowell."

Jake shrugged and started for the door.

"Where are you going?" Thompson asked.

"Somewhere you won't hear me talking, Lieutenant." Jake infused his tone with the right amount of respect because he truly liked the older man and knew his superior had the department's as well as Jake's best interests at heart.

"I hear you in my sleep," Lieutenant Thompson muttered, and Jake laughed, letting the door swing shut behind him.

In the stale-smelling hall, he slowed his steps, taking in what he knew so far. His perp was playing clean until he figured the cops were through with him. And though Lieutenant Thompson might know Jake was sniffing around, at least he now thought Jake was cooperating with therapy. He wouldn't be too hard on him if he caught Jake looking into things behind the scenes. With his live-in therapist at work from nine to five, Jake had his daytime free to hunt around.

And he had his nights free for Brianne.

BRIANNE TRIPPED on her shoelace and paused in front of the high-rise building that housed Rina's penthouse on the Upper East Side of Manhattan. Jimmy had moved her in yesterday, and, to her surprise, Jake had made himself scarce. He'd shown her to her room, told her to make herself at home, and then left her to settle in, saying he had an appointment. She appreciated the respect and space he'd given her to acclimate alone to her new surroundings. When Jake was in there, the humongous apartment grew much smaller, and there seemed to be no air to breathe.

As she knelt down to tie her shoe, a humid breeze blew in the night, similar to the air that wafted through her window as she tried to sleep. Because the air-conditioning in the penthouse was cool and uncomfortable, and she'd hoped some familiarity would help her relax, she'd opened the window last night seeking the warmer air. But she'd tossed and turned, anyway, restless because of a heat that had nothing to do with Norton lying next to her or the outside temperature, and everything to do with the fire Jake ignited in her.

She double-knotted the lace, lingering over the simple task, avoiding going "home." But eventually she had no choice. She stood, smoothing her dark green hospital scrubs and taking a deep breath for courage before facing Jake. She deliberately hadn't changed after work, hoping the more professional she looked, the more professional she'd act. Even if Jake forced her to tease and cajole him into some form of cooperation, she planned to maintain distance.

It would take strength and fortitude not to succumb to her attraction to Jake, but she'd gathered that strength before, at the lowest point in her life. She'd just have to gather it again. Rina's job gave her a means of achieving goals—the money to relocate to California and to continue to be close to the brother she'd raised.

Giving in to Jake's seductive powers, succumbing to a man who valued danger and risk, couldn't result in anything more than a short-term affair. Brianne didn't indulge in meaningless relationships. She'd learned long ago that they failed to relieve the loneliness. And given the strength of the attraction between herself and Jake, by indulging she would only set herself up for a broken heart.

BRIANNE NELSON. Pretty name for a pretty lady, Louis thought. A name he'd had no trouble learning from the waitresses at the upscale bar Detective Lowell liked to frequent. Louis Ramirez wasn't surprised a man like Lowell had developed an interest in the woman. Any red-blooded man would look twice. *He* had. And now she was bent over, tying her shoes, giving him a view of her slim waist and rounded ass. What a waste, her interest in the detective.

The damn cop thought he was so smart. Louis couldn't stifle the snicker that escaped. He'd not only beaten the rap, he'd beaten Lowell. Lowell hadn't been clever enough to recognize a setup. He'd gotten shot and hadn't been strong enough to pull himself up and do the Miranda rights himself. And he hadn't been able to keep Louis in jail. Louis loved the cop's obvious frustration over the fact that no one could say Louis was anything but a clean citizen now. But talking to Louis's girlfriend was taking things too far. Making things too personal.

Personal could go both ways, he thought, and watched as Brianne Nelson headed into Lowell's building and checked in at the security desk out front. Fancy address for a cop to be hanging out. He took a drag on his cigarette, then stomped it into the ground. Lowell was a damn fool if he trusted money to keep him safe. Because if and when the time came, no doorman or security system would keep Louis out.

# 4

JAKE SPENT THE AFTERNOON on the streets talking to old informants and even older friends. No one had any information on Ramirez, but Jake hadn't expected them to. All he wanted was for the slime to know he was on the prowl, asking questions. That he hadn't forgotten Ramirez had taken down a cop, was responsible for Jake's injury. That they would meet up again.

When Jake got home, the apartment was quiet except for Norton. Though Jake wanted nothing more than to hit the shower and relax, he grabbed the leash and took the dog on a long walk—on the hot sidewalk. The pedigreed pooch dragged his heels, trying to run home or bolt into any open door he could find where the sun wasn't baking the concrete. No mutt with a brain would want to roast in this heat, and Norton obviously agreed. Jake had to admit, the dog was smart, something the sharpei had proven when he'd rolled over and begged for a belly rub from Brianne. Figuring they had in common both their attraction to her and the fact that they both were male, he decided to give the dog a break.

Once Jake got Norton to his favorite patch of grass, he gave the order his sister had explained would take care of things fast. "Do business," Jake muttered, hoping nobody saw him talking to the mutt.

Unbelievably, as usual, Norton finally did his thing.

Jake rewarded him with a fast trip home and a huge bowl of cold water. Then he took a cool shower for himself, and by the time he heard the sounds of Brianne's return, he'd washed away the grime of the day. He was ready to spar with Brianne, to keep her at a respectable enough distance to avoid therapy—among other physical entanglements he couldn't afford.

Jake told himself that his moral code wouldn't let him take advantage of their living situation. He reminded himself that putting Ramirez away had to come first. And he knew for certain that being both a cop and a gentleman who kept his hands off Brianne would require all his mental and physical energy.

He stepped back and greeted her in the large marble entryway. "Welcome home."

With a curt nod, she walked toward him with brisk, no-nonsense steps. Obviously she had the same concept of distance in mind. He forcibly stopped his smile from turning into a full-fledged grin. Her curt stride, accompanied by her baggy green pants and top exuded a professional demeanor, one she no doubt intended to use to put him off.

He understood. He'd tossed and turned last night, knowing she was asleep in another room in the same apartment, remembering the kiss and knowing he would have liked to take it further—to make love to her and satisfy the yearning she inspired.

She stopped in front of him and let out a huge sigh. "Boy, am I beat."

Before Jake could respond, Norton bolted into the room and ran across the floor, coming to a sliding halt in front of her. If she hadn't been in his way, he'd have hit the elevator doors behind her with a resounding *thud.*

Brianne grinned and bent down to scratch behind his ear. "Hiya, Norton. How are you? I missed you today."

Jake groaned. Leave it to the mutt to thaw the chill. He wished she'd missed him half as much—then realized he was jealous of the dog. He shook his head, as disgusted with himself as he was impressed with Brianne, an exhausted woman with a soft spot for a lonely pet.

"I'm sure he missed you, too. With Rina gone, he's at loose ends. He either whines nonstop, or I can't find him anywhere. Like last night. I think he must've curled up somewhere that reminded him of Rina. A pile of clothes or someplace I haven't found yet." He shrugged with his one good shoulder.

"He was with me."

He glanced up, surprised. An adorable smile tugged at her lips.

"He weighs a ton. I couldn't move, couldn't roll over. Once he lay down next to me on my blanket, I couldn't budge him, not even with all my body weight. I'm sure you know what I'm talking about since he must have slept with you before I moved in."

"No, he sat at the foot of the bed whining all night." Jake shook his head and swallowed hard. He couldn't believe what he was hearing. While he'd lain awake fantasizing about Brianne, the damn dog had been living Jake's dreams. He eyed Norton, who lay at her feet, with an annoyed scowl.

"Really? Hmm." She stretched and yawned all at the same time and quickly clasped an embarrassed hand over her mouth. "I'm sorry. I'm just low on energy. Add to that the tossing and turning I tried to do last night and…well…sorry.'' A beautiful blush stained her cheeks. "I'm just tired. And hungry.''

In that instant, Jake decided everything, including being jealous of Norton and keeping his distance, could wait. She appeared more exhausted than he'd remembered seeing her. Then again, he hadn't had too many up-close-and-personal conversations, something that would change now that they lived under one roof. Looking at her tired face, he had a very strong desire to wrap Brianne in his arms and keep her safe—from the outside world, and from her own life which was so obviously wearing on her.

As a cop, he'd always had an overactive protective instinct, but what he felt now went beyond a professional impulse to protect. "Can I get you anything to drink? A glass of soda or water?'' he asked.

She shook her head. "No, thanks. Just food. I know we never discussed the details of this living arrangement, but I did some food shopping during my lunch hour and I thought I'd put together a quick dinner. Can I…should I…'' Her voice trailed off, professionalism giving way to uncertainty, barriers crumbling in light of awkward reality.

He found her uncertainty endearing and a refreshing change from her consummate forced demeanor. To hell with the cop and his secrets, Jake thought. The man in him wanted to ease her stress. "Actually, I called in for pizza before jumping into the shower. It's already in the kitchen. You're welcome to share.''

"Thank you. I *love* pizza and, to be honest, I'm so exhausted, cooking's the last thing I want to do.'' Her enthusiasm was so tangible he wanted to taste it—and her.

She turned, her ponytail bobbing as she bounded toward the kitchen, Norton hot on her trail. Jake followed a short distance behind. She tossed a canvas bag on the floor by one of Rina's decorator wrought-iron, ladder-back kitchen chairs, rested her hands on the table, and inhaled deeply.

"Mmm. That smells delicious. I haven't had a slice in ages."

"How come?"

She turned to face him. "How come what?"

"If you love pizza so much, why haven't you had any lately? You work two jobs, long hours, and you said yourself you're exhausted. Every single New Yorker knows take-out's easier than cooking."

"It also gets expensive."

He debated for a moment, then decided to ask. "Two jobs must bring in a good salary. What does the money go for, if you don't mind my asking?" Once again, it wasn't the cop's need for answers but personal curiosity that drove him now. A need to get to know her better.

She eased herself into a chair, her hands curling around the gleaming chrome handles. "My parents died when I was twenty. My brother was nine, and I've raised him ever since."

Her lonely existence touched the heart he'd closed off after his ex-wife left. "I'm sorry."

He came up beside her, placing what he meant to be a supportive hand on her shoulder. But when it came to Brianne, no touch was simple. Heat exploded beneath his fingertips, but he left his hand in place, unable and unwilling to break contact.

"It's been a long time, but thanks. Marc, my brother, he's special, unbelievably bright, and it would have been a disservice to him and his abilities to keep him in public school. Everything I earn has been split between his education and making ends meet.''

Jake stared, grateful for the insight and amazed at her generous spirit. She'd given and sacrificed everything for her sibling, and, though Jake would do the same for Rina, his heart twisted with the notion that he'd been right—Brianne was an incredible woman. ''Your brother's lucky to have you.''

A blush rose to her cheeks, and she waved away the compliment, as if what she'd done was inconsequential. ''I'm lucky to have him. We're like this—'' She crossed her fingers to make her point.

He nodded, an unexpected lump in his throat. ''Well, dig in.'' He pointed to the white pizza box on the table. ''Your days of deprivation are at an end.''

She grinned and did as he asked. For the duration of the short meal, he watched more than he ate, gaining his fill from her satisfied sighs and gratitude. Such a simple thing, and it broke down barriers far more than any come-on ever would. It was progress he hadn't expected and it touched him more than he would have liked, especially for a man who couldn't afford any involvement or distractions right now.

She wiped her mouth with a paper napkin and rose to clean the table. Used to fending for himself, Jake helped and, despite the size of the large kitchen, they bumped into one another often, the current between them charged.

Still, by the time she'd disposed of the garbage and turned back to him, she seemed calmer and more composed than he felt at the moment. ''Ready to work?'' she asked.

Professional, he thought again. But nothing could

erase the confidence she'd shared or the heat they generated. Hell, he'd already caught the fragrant strawberry scent he associated with this woman—the one that turned him inside out and made him *want* more than he could put into words. But she was right. She was here to do a job, and he ought to let her do it.

"Ready to try and convince me?" He grinned. "It's a gorgeous night out. Want to see the stars?"

"Pathetic pickup line," she said.

He chuckled. "No joke. The whirlpool's outside." He deliberately waited a beat. "Under the stars."

Although she blushed a furious shade of red, she held her ground and his gaze. He was still hoping to persuade her to get some rest, but if she insisted on working, he figured sexual innuendo would keep her on her guard—and at a distance. He couldn't trust himself if they got too close, and heaven help him if her hands actually worked on his body. This woman could have him forgetting his own name, never mind Ramirez.

"It's the whirlpool or the tub in the master bath," he said lightly, referring to the water therapy she'd mentioned the other day.

She picked up her duffel bag. "I'll need to see the extent of your injury and mobility before I can even think about the type of exercises you'll need. Are you going to let me evaluate you?"

"Wouldn't you rather take it easy? You said yourself you're exhausted." Although he had to admit, the food had put color back in her cheeks and she didn't look as tired as she had earlier. He wondered if the sexual innuendo had anything to do with the flush in her face and the sudden energy.

"Nice stalling tactic, but it won't work. Give me a

chance, okay? First we'll loosen the area with wet heat wrapped around your shoulder, and then I'll check your mobility."

"Wet heat, huh? Sounds interesting." His gaze dropped to her lips. She'd licked them once and did so again, her nerves clearly showing despite her outward calm. And just thinking about breaching those walls again, this time feeling her melt in his arms, at his touch, did something to him deep inside.

"Moist heating pads," she explained, "on the affected area." If she'd been flustered before, the blush and body shifting increased now. "You know what I mean."

"Yes, I do." He let out a mock long-suffering sigh. "No whirlpool?"

"I said water therapy's always an option. I didn't say I'd be using it on you." She wagged her finger in front of him, scolding him for jumping to conclusions.

"What if I'm a good boy and cooperate? Then do I get the water treatment?" He offered her a pleading look and got a laugh for his effort.

Jake knew one thing for certain. No matter how much of a distraction she'd be, he wanted her in that whirlpool willingly before the summer was through. Not that he planned to give in to the need. Still, he reached for her, wrapping his palm around that finger. Surprised, her gaze met his, and his breath caught in his throat. Those warm, compelling green eyes turned the tables, giving her the control that should have been his.

He'd never been in danger of losing control before. Even when his tumultuous marriage was at its best and most sexually charged, he'd never experienced the chemistry he felt now, had never felt the desire to cede power and see where it took him.

She swallowed hard. "Tell you what. You cooperate, and I'll *consider* the whirlpool."

"Hardly a fair deal."

"But it does give you something to work toward, doesn't it? In case returning mobility isn't enough of a motivator." She met and held his gaze, assessing him. She took his measure, and, as she studied him, Jake knew he had a formidable adversary. One he wouldn't be able to con for long.

He let out a slow groan. He couldn't just walk away, and eventually he'd either be confiding in her and asking her to keep his secret or he'd be dead meat, his plan for the summer and Ramirez busted before it began. "Okay, then. I guess the gym would be the best place to start?"

"You have a gym?"

She wiggled her finger free, and he let her go. For now. "This place has all sorts of amenities. Rina didn't show you?"

Brianne shook her head. "Not the gym."

"I was hoping she'd venture back into that room again. But it was her husband's favorite spot and it brings back too many memories." Brianne's eyes softened in understanding, and Jake let out a groan. "Come." He grasped her bag with his good arm, ignoring her glare, feeling certain she wouldn't get into a tug-of-war with a patient.

He gestured for her to follow, turned and headed for the incredible home gym his brother-in-law had created, stopping in the doorway. Large windows covered the walls and sunlight bounced off the chrome, state-of-the-art equipment. Where there were no windows there were floor-to-ceiling mirrors instead.

Brianne came up beside him. He sensed her presence, felt her body heat, and his own temperature rose in response.

"Nice setup," she murmured.

"Personally I prefer the Village Gym." He turned and saw how impressed she was. "My brother-in-law was more into glitz than necessity, but I can't deny it's perfect for what we need." And the only room in this whole apartment where he felt completely at ease.

"You don't live here." It wasn't a question, and he wasn't surprised she'd drawn the correct conclusion. The papers he'd given her outlined his injury and how it was sustained. Common sense dictated a cop couldn't afford such luxury.

"Disappointed?" He wished he'd withheld the bitterness from his voice, but the past still lived within him.

He'd met his ex-wife, Linda, at the city school where she'd been teaching, when he'd shown up for a talk to the kids about the hazards of drug use. They'd hit it off fast, sharing incredible chemistry, great sex and seemingly similar goals and desires. She'd seemed to be in awe of his badge and uniform, and had been more than happy to marry a cop with a steady income, if unpredictable hours. They both wanted to move out of the city, Linda so she could teach in a safer neighborhood, and Jake so he could enjoy a peaceful family life during his off-time.

But as soon as the honeymoon ended, everything she'd seemed to like and accept in Jake underwent a radical shift. His hours suddenly became too long compared to her friend's professional husbands, while the money Jake made was insufficient for decorating the home they'd bought in the suburbs. Jake wasn't a man who liked to overspend or overextend his credit, and for damn sure his salary hadn't been able to support his wife's sudden desire to stay at home and shop with the wealthier women she'd met in the area. She sure as hell hadn't been able to deal with Rina and Robert's luxurious lifestyle. Jake's marriage had lasted three increasingly bitter years—years in which he and his wife grew further and further apart. She finally walked out.

Jake hadn't realized that the past still haunted him so strongly, until faced with the possibility that Brianne might find him and his lifestyle lacking. Despite her willingness to sacrifice for her brother, why wouldn't Brianne be impressed with this penthouse and disappointed that Jake wasn't its owner?

"Am I disappointed you don't own this place?" she asked.

"Or have the money to live here," he muttered.

"That's ridiculous. It's not like I was after you for money." What sounded like genuine hurt laced her tone. "It's not like I was after you at all."

Jake chose not to touch that statement, picking up on her emotion instead. He wanted to keep his distance, not hurt her in the process. "My comment was uncalled for."

"Is that your masculine way of saying 'I'm sorry'?" She faced him, her back to the door frame, her hands braced behind her.

He reached out and tucked a stray curl behind her ear. "It's my way of saying I'm an ass."

"I couldn't have put it better myself." She laughed, and her breasts pushed temptingly against the soft cotton uniform she wore, rising and falling with each breath she took.

For a moment, the barriers she'd put up between them were gone, making him want to reach out to her, to hold her in his arms and... Without warning, gut-level fear took hold. He'd had his heart ripped to shreds over his lifestyle and his lack of money once before. He couldn't go there again.

Although he had no idea how much money Rina was paying Brianne for her services, for her sacrifice—moving in and devoting her nights—he had no doubt she was being well compensated. And though Brianne's reasons for needing money were altruistic and good, it didn't mean that once she'd finished caring for her brother she wouldn't desire more in life than she'd had before. And "more" demanded money, something a cop would never have in abundance.

"Would you believe I'm apartment- and dog-sitting for the summer?"

"Of course. You've been set up, just like me." He didn't miss the bitterness in her tone.

Obviously her anger at Rina hadn't dissipated, and he couldn't say he blamed her.

"Speaking of dog-sitting and setups, we need to keep him out of here so neither of us trip."

Jake nodded, and because Norton had curled up in his crate while they ate, he was able to shut the gym door without creating a scene.

"Is there a sink in here?" Brianne asked next.

He nodded. "There's a full bathroom back that way." He gestured to the closed door across the room.

"How about a..."

"There's a massage area in the corner," he said,

reading her mind. "Trust me, there's nothing you'll need that you won't find here."

She shook her head, her auburn ponytail falling over one shoulder. "Amazing."

He clenched his fists to avoid giving in to the impulse to twirl her hair around his fingers...and feel the silken strands brushing over other aware body parts. Instead he focused on their surroundings and her reaction to them. "It's called wealth, so enjoy it while it's at your disposal."

"If you say so." Her smile was wary.

She grabbed the bag he'd deposited at his feet and headed for the bathroom. Soon the sound of running water reached his ears. His vision of wet heat involved slick bodies—hers and his—in the shower, out of the shower... He didn't care as long as they were creating that moist, intense heat.

Friction and pleasure, he thought, and his body shook in reaction. He had to get himself in check. He couldn't plan strategy or figure out how to keep her in the dark about his ability to move well until he got a feel for what she had in store. Jake had no idea what Brianne's idea of therapy entailed, but he was about to find out.

BRIANNE CLOSED HERSELF in the bathroom and breathed deeply. She splashed cold water on her face before setting up her equipment for Jake. She re-entered the room, hoping she was more in control of her physical reactions to him. But she took one look at him fully clothed, realized she hadn't told him to undress for therapy, and accepted that, given their situation, she'd rarely be in control.

She sighed, bracing herself for the inevitable. "If

we're going to do this right, you need to take off your shirt."

As he reached for the hem of his ragged sweatshirt with one hand, Jake's eyes sparkled with mischief. He looked like a man who was about to be given his fondest wish, or rather a man who thought he was about to give her her fondest wish, by stripping down in her presence.

"Get a grip, Don Juan. It's a purely professional request. I can't very well heat your shoulder if you're wearing heavy cotton."

He laughed, obviously not the least bit offended. "Are you saying you don't want to see my bare chest?"

"I've seen enough bare-chested men in my career. I'm sure yours is no different from the rest." She averted her gaze before he could see the lie in her eyes. His bare chest was spectacular.

"You wound me."

This time she laughed, but at the sound of his groan—definitely one of pain—she pivoted back toward him in time to see him grimace as he began to remove his shirt with his good hand, with more help than she'd expected from his injured side.

She wondered what was going on. "You said you haven't been in therapy."

He averted his eyes. "I never actually said that. I have a friend in physical therapy who gave me some exercises and checks in once in a while. I've been working the shoulder some."

She wasn't yet sure how much exercise he had or hadn't been doing, but after a session with him, she would. "*Some* exercise isn't enough."

He treated her to a sexy wink. "That's why I have you."

"I'm only as good as your willingness to follow through, and you haven't guaranteed me anything yet."

"I'm not worried."

"Well, I am." She stepped forward, intending to get past the word games and get started on the therapy. "If I'm so good, then let me help you get that shirt off."

He narrowed his eyes, and Brianne could see the war going on inside him. She'd seen it many times before. Allow help and look weak or continue the struggle alone. Normally she'd let the internal struggle go on until the patient gave in, but she sensed Jake wasn't one to cave easily. She now understood the reason for the cutoff sweatshirts. They allowed him wide sleeve room, easier movement.

She had every intention of returning him to full mobility, even if she had to play up to his masculine ego in order to maintain his cooperation. "Come on, Jake. I'm really good with my hands." Her voice dropped to a husky level despite her best intentions.

"I just bet you are." His eyes darkened as he spoke, his voice a deep rumble that set her nerve endings on fire. Her goals, the reasons why she shouldn't give in to this attraction, diluted each time he got within touching distance.

Reaching out, she grabbed for the hem of his shirt, her fingers grazing his warm skin. At the contact, his stomach muscles rippled beneath her touch, and he sucked in an audible, affected breath. She understood. Her body reacted in an intimate, sexual way, too. Need curled deep in her belly, and her nipples pulled into tight peaks as if awaiting a lover's caress.

Never in her career had a patient session resonated with desire, and her hands shook as she lifted his shirt up and over his head, exposing that exceptional bare chest for view. Heat emanated from his body to hers, drawing her in, enticing her to drop her guard and shed her inhibitions.

She dropped his shirt instead. And though instinct told her to take a safe step back, she was drawn to him in ways she didn't understand and ways she wanted to explore more deeply. Slowly, so she didn't hurt him, she smoothed her palm over his bruised flesh. He let out a drawn-out groan, a rumble that reverberated inside her, and his hands came up to cradle her cheeks. "When you touch me it feels so damn good."

Her heart beat rapidly in her chest. "It's my job to make you feel better." And it was her job to pull away from him—but the connection was too strong, the need to be with him too compelling.

"Then, by all means, do your best." His thumb brushed back and forth over her skin, caressing her face.

Unable to resist, she leaned forward and placed a gentle kiss on the least bruised part of his chest, over his warm flesh.

"Brianne." Her name came out both as a warning and a plea.

The next thing she knew his lips were on hers—or had her lips come to his? She didn't know, but everything between them was real and mutual, hot and ravenous. His tongue delved inside her mouth with passion and need, taking all she offered and giving even more. He smoothed one hand down her back and over her buttocks, pausing there, stopping to knead her flesh through the barrier of clothing and to pull her so close she could feel his hard erection straining against the confines of his jeans.

He wanted her. Not that she'd doubted it before—how could she, with the heated stares and longing glances?—but she felt it now and the certainty fueled bravery she hadn't known she possessed. She trailed a path with her tongue from his lips to his cheek and outward, lingering behind his ear and nibbling on his earlobe until his large, masculine body trembled in response to her touch.

She inhaled, and his heady scent enveloped her, making her feel, for the first time in her life, that she wasn't alone. Desire exploded in waves, curling in her stomach, wrapping around her heart and causing her to crave so much more than the fiery touches they'd shared so far. She wanted to feel his bare skin covering hers, needed him inside her to fill the aching emptiness she'd carried for so long. It was an ache that she sensed only he could satisfy.

And that was the thought that brought her to her senses and forced her to break their electric connection and step back, away from the fire. *He* was the one person who could take her to soaring heights—and destroy her dreams. Better to concentrate on her tangible goals—finishing this job, being with her brother, moving to California.

"Wow." Not exactly a sophisticated response, but Brianne was so shaken up that she couldn't formulate a better response.

"That about says it." Jake ran a trembling hand through his hair. "You okay?"

He eyed her with a concern she didn't want to see or feel. Not from him, a man who was the antithesis of everything she desired in life, and that could be summed up in one word: safe.

She nodded. "Fine. I'm fine," she lied. "You?"

A sexy grin curved his lips. "Touch me again and I'll be even better."

"I was asking about the pain in your shoulder." Two lies in two minutes. And after all her hard work teaching Marc the value of honesty, she thought wryly.

"If you say so. Look, Brianne, about what just happened…"

She shook her head. "Forget about it. It was bound to happen and it's already forgotten." Another whopper for the books. She'd never forget how warm and welcoming his mouth felt on hers, never truly put his touch behind her. "Let's just get back to work, shall we? Sit down, and I'll be right back."

To her surprise, he complied, shifting in the leather chair until he found a comfortable position. His gaze never left hers, challenging her. She had a hunch that his sudden cooperation was for her benefit because he sensed how thrown she still was. Brianne didn't care about the reason; she was just grateful not to have to spar or argue with him at the moment, and she desperately needed a minute alone.

Ducking into the bathroom, she exhaled deeply and splashed cold water over her face—again. Looking in the mirror, she took in her bright eyes and flushed cheeks. Everything she felt was mirrored in her expression—the desire, the longing. But she couldn't indulge further any more than she could hide in here forever. Yet, as she headed back into the room, she knew even her coat of professional armor wouldn't help her now.

Five minutes later, she had a still-cooperative Jake settled in his seat, wet heat cushioning his neck and shoulders—much the way she desired to cradle him in her arms and ease his pain, she thought, recalling the way he'd winced as she'd positioned him with the padding. Curling her hands around the edge of hard leather, she perched on the seat of a workout machine, dangling her feet while the heat worked on his shoulder.

Silence surrounded them, and his intense, serious gaze never left hers. She wondered what he was thinking, how that kiss had affected him, and knew she couldn't afford to find out, not if she intended to walk away unscathed.

"So how'd you sustain this injury?" She sought conversation that would distract her still-tingling body and remind her of all the reasons she couldn't let herself get involved with this cop who thrived on danger.

He leaned his head back against the headrest as if debating what to tell her. "We got a tip on a drug dealer we'd been watching," he said finally. "Figured we'd catch him in the act. This was a key chance to get him off the street."

As he spoke, his eyes began to glitter with remembered determination. He obviously liked his job and fed on the rush of getting the bad guys. Even as disappointment filled her, so did unexpected admiration for the man and his work. She might not like what he did for a living, but how could she not respect it? And him?

"Turns out it was a setup. Our guy showed—with company. Took out a damn good cop. Frank was my football buddy and best friend. A decent guy with a wife and kids. Meanwhile, I hit the ground, he took the bullet, I fractured the shoulder diving out of the way and got shot, anyway. But if I hadn't gone down, if I'd taken Frank's bullet, those kids would still have a father,'' he muttered.

''And your already grieving sister would have lost another loved one. Don't question fate,'' she said, although she'd done just that, many times in her overworked, solitary life.

''I take it I should be grateful I just got hit by a bullet and ended up with a bum shoulder?''

She winced at his nonchalant description. Proof that danger was so much a part of him, he remained unfazed even after injury. ''There are other ways of saying it.''

''Maybe. But *Uncle* Jake is hardly a fair trade-off to those kids.''

He was right, but the thought of his being killed didn't sit well with her. ''Everyone has someone who cares about them. You wouldn't want Rina to experience that pain again. Sometimes you just have to accept and move on.''

His assessing stare never wavered. ''It would have been easier if the guy had been caught and put away. But, to top off the night, some rookie grabbed the perp first and screwed up his Miranda rights,'' he said in disgust. ''The slime walked on a technicality.''

She nodded, noting his clenched jaw and deciding it was time to change the subject once more. But she still wanted to steer clear of that kiss and her growing feelings for Jake, the man. His caring about his partner's family added another dimension to his person-

ality, this one warmer and decidedly vulnerable,
though she doubted he'd ever admit to it.

"So tell me. Why have you been giving Rina a hard
time about therapy?" Brianne had her doubts that he
was as immobile as his sister believed, and she wondered what exactly was going on with Jake Lowell.

Gratitude for the topic switch flitted across his expression and then was gone. "And here I thought I
was being a model patient." His blue eyes met hers,
daring her to disagree.

"I admit you're cooperating right now. But obviously you hadn't been, since Rina was worried enough
to hire me."

"You already know physical therapy wasn't the
only reason Rina hired you," he reminded her. "Not
that I'm defending my sister, but she can't stop herself
from looking out for me. She lost her husband several
months ago and I'm all she has left."

His voice deepened, and Brianne couldn't help feel
his obvious love and concern for his sister. The softer
part of him showed once more and beckoned to her in
a way that threatened her ability to maintain distance.
His caring for others—Frank's family and his sister—
was something she could relate to. She shivered at the
notion because their kiss proved she was already having a tough time steering clear of the connection between them. The more they had in common, the harder
it was to remain unaffected by him. *California, a stable existence, a life of my own,* she reminded herself.
She could have none of those if she got involved with
Jake.

Jake watched Brianne closely. Her wariness didn't
surprise him. Hell, after that explosive kiss he was
pretty uptight himself.

Twice now they'd proven that each time they got together, they ended in a clinch neither expected and neither could control. Not good for a man who'd promised himself he'd maintain distance and a clear head. But around Brianne, distance was impossible and so was rational thinking. Just knowing he'd put personal restrictions against being with this woman made him more frustrated and uptight than he could ever remember being.

"Rina needs you," Brianne said, bringing him back to the present. "All the more reason for you to forget the guilt and be glad you're alive—for your sister's sake." Her eyes flickered with banked emotion.

Jake would learn to live with the guilt, as soon as he had Ramirez behind bars. He cleared his throat. "Well, Rina doesn't need to worry. I'm fine, and you'll be able to tell her that as soon as she returns."

"I'll tell her the truth. If you cooperate, she'll know that. If you give me a hard time, she'll hear about that, too."

And that was exactly what bothered him about this deal Rina had made with Brianne. He couldn't have Brianne reporting his cooperation back to the woman who paid her salary, or Brianne working on his shoulder and discovering exactly how mobile he actually was. Either way, Jake was in deep.

She swung her feet back and forth. "You do realize you can't afford to fool around, not if you want full range of motion back."

The telephone rang and Brianne jumped, obviously startled by the unexpected interruption. Bound by heating pads, Jake motioned toward the portable phone set up in the corner. "Would you get that for me?"

She nodded and brought the handset to him.

"Lowell."

"It's Duke. A guy ODed on some bad shit. The girlfriend's in critical condition. It's Vickers's case, but he called me. Nothing coherent's come out of her yet and the hospital's restricted her visitors, but they promised as soon as it was okay they'd give us a go-ahead to talk to her. It's possible we can piece together some kind of lead on Ramirez once she comes to."

"Pick me up in five."

"If the lieutenant finds out you're sniffing around an active case and a potential witness…"

"So don't tell him." Jake slammed down the phone and found himself face-to-face with Brianne's wide, curious, gorgeous green eyes.

"No therapy?"

He'd walked out on women before, but, damn, why did the disappointment in this one's tone hit him like a punch in the gut? He shook his head. "Something's come up." And he couldn't tell her a thing.

"I thought you were off duty. On leave."

He let out a groan. "I am. This is…about my friend's family. The one I just told you about. One of the kids is having a problem…"

"Say no more." She jumped up and began to unwrap the heating pads from his back and shoulder. "You don't owe me a detailed explanation. I don't like it, but this can wait." Understanding and compassion filled her expression, making Jake feel like a first-class heel for lying and for ducking out on her.

She understood and didn't question. Even his ex-wife had never done that. Everything he'd worried about and sought to avoid since Rina's revelation about inviting Brianne to live here was coming to pass.

"Thanks." He shook his head, not knowing what else to say.

"Take care of your friend's family." Brianne knelt down and tossed him his shirt.

He slipped the wide-necked cutoff over his head, and his arms followed. He struggled a bit and winced slightly, but not nearly as much as he should have, Jake realized when he caught Brianne's knowing gaze.

Arms folded over her chest, foot tapping against the floor, she looked at him and frowned. "When you get back we can talk about your real need for therapy. And your so-called need for me."

# 5

JAKE NEEDED BRIANNE. Needed her in his bed. Needed her in his life. Needed an affair that wouldn't deny him everything about her he desired. Mostly he had to get the woman out of his system before his obsession with her completely consumed him.

He'd been standing at the crime scene watching Forensics work. If he wasn't good friends with the guys on duty he'd have been tossed out on his ass, but they'd let him stay as they picked through the remnants of a romantic dinner gone wrong. Yet, instead of focusing on details, Jake had been thinking of Brianne.

When he'd seen the half-empty glasses of wine, he'd envisioned her taking a seductive sip, licking the fruity liquid off her lips and letting him taste it on her tongue. And when he'd gotten a glimpse of the leftovers from dinner, he'd been remembering Brianne's nearly orgasmic groans of satisfaction while eating a simple slice of pizza. He'd been so wrapped up in memories and what could be that he'd nearly missed an important piece of evidence, one the detectives hadn't gotten to yet.

Wrappers from a place called The Eclectic Eatery, the sister restaurant to a place that originally had opened in the Village, had littered the table. Nothing unusual about take-out garbage from the newest trendy hot spot frequented by grad students, Jake thought. But beside them lay what looked like dinner mints—colored candy-like mints that probably weren't—lying out in plain sight. But there was no proof the goods came from The Eclectic Eatery.

Seconds after Jake pointed out the scattered pieces, the gloved Forensics guys had bagged the candy or pills or whatever the hell they were. But one of the tablets had a designer signature similar to the one Ramirez used on his goods. Thanks to Louis's overblown ego, he'd overestimated his own intelligence and had had a stamp made that identified his goods instead of using the generic labels other dealers relied upon. Jake had had no doubt the scum would get back into business. He'd just figured the guy would be smart enough to change his M.O.

Exactly the argument Duke was using. He believed it was a copycat looking to cash in on Ramirez's clientele. But Jake just knew the goods came from Louis. The man's arrogance would eventually do him in, and this was just the beginning. At least now they had a lead. Jake could watch The Eclectic Eatery and see if Ramirez showed his face, find out if the new restaurant was a front for selling drugs. It was a lead Jake might never have found if his head had remained in the clouds, fantasizing about Brianne. True, Forensics would probably have uncovered the pills, but Jake had seen them first. He needed to remember that his job ought to come first as well.

Unfortunately, Jake knew exactly where his lack of concentration came from. He was obsessed with a woman he'd promised would remain forbidden. But with thoughts of her distracting him and jeopardizing his case, he could no longer tell himself an affair would only get in the way. In fact, an affair, the last thing he'd thought he wanted, might be the only solution, the only means to get Brianne out of his system once and for all and clear his head for the job at hand. Back-assed reasoning, he knew. But a possible solution, nonetheless.

And there was another upside to an affair with Brianne. He could keep an eye on her better and know her whereabouts easier if they were indulging in an intimate relationship. Ramirez demanded his full concentration, and if he wasn't distracted by what-if thoughts of Brianne, Jake could give the case his all.

He could give Brianne his all at the same time. Frank's death had driven home how short life was. The time he'd wasted avoiding Brianne at the café could have been better spent acting on his desire. It wasn't too late. If Brianne agreed with his reasoning, the Ramirez case would build toward completion at the same time that his obsession with Brianne began to fade. Both would end and he'd walk away at the end of the summer. Toward what, though, he didn't yet know.

But would she agree? The way she'd melted in his arms told him her desire flared as quickly and as hot as his, but she'd backed off just as fast. With a little luck and persuasion he could convince her to indulge in a summer fling. He had to. His sanity depended on it.

When he returned to the penthouse, he wasn't surprised to find the living room and kitchen dark, but he was disappointed, nonetheless. Even Norton didn't bound out to meet him, and Jake figured the dog was in Brianne's bed—exactly where he wanted to be.

How much more pathetic could things get? he wondered, stifling a wry laugh.

But as he made his way to his room, he discovered the lights on in the gym. Jake peered inside. Brianne had obviously just finished a workout and stood wiping down her arms, neck and forehead. True to form, Norton had settled in a corner, content to alternately sleep and watch Brianne—something Jake could relate to. Except that when he looked at Brianne, sleep was the last thing on his mind. Tight black leggings encased her long legs and a brief exercise top covered her chest, ending just below her full breasts, exposing peaked nipples, a flat belly and pale skin.

Molten heat seared his body, and Jake swallowed hard, unable to pull his gaze from the unexpected, tempting sight.

She patted her forehead, then lowered the towel and glanced up, catching his stare as he stood in the doorway. "I didn't hear you come in. Is everything okay?" she asked.

"Yes." He stepped into the room. "No. I need to talk to you."

She inclined her head and gestured to the bench near one of the mirrored walls. "Come sit." She patted the seat beside her.

He swallowed hard, then joined her.

"You've had more than a little therapy." She jumped to the natural assumption after she'd witnessed his ability to put on his shirt with relative ease. "With the help you've been getting you don't need me." She started to rise, and he clamped a hand over her wrist to keep her next to him.

"Yes, Brianne, I do."

She lowered herself slowly. Her green eyes raked

over his face, searching for answers. "What are you saying?"

"I need more therapy."

"Just not as much as everyone thinks."

He gave a short nod. "Can I trust you to keep my secret?"

"You have my word."

Even as she spoke, he realized he hadn't had to ask. She'd respect his request. Her dedication to her brother spoke of her character, and his gut told him even more. He'd always trusted his instincts before. He had no reason not to now.

He squeezed her hand tight. "I've made progress with the rehab. A lot more than Rina, or the department, thinks."

"But why keep your progress a secret?"

"I have my reasons." Reasons he couldn't share. Not only because he was unofficially working on a case but because her safety depended on her not knowing details. Another reason an affair would work. He could keep her safe by getting inside her head and by knowing where she was at all times.

She shifted, sliding so close that the heat of her body and the scent of her femininity surrounded him. His adrenaline pumped harder as he formulated what he could reveal. "Some of my reasons have to do with general life dissatisfaction and some are more personal. I can't divulge them but..."

"Shh." She placed a finger over his lips, and he found her touch warm, soft and gentle. "You don't owe me explanations. It's not like you're the one who hired me."

"But I am the one who wants to keep you."

Brianne let out the breath she hadn't been aware of

holding. If he didn't need or want therapy, if he didn't need her, Rina's money and Brianne's plans for a future would disappear before her eyes. Relief that she didn't have to worry about losing this job…relief that she wouldn't be losing Jake, yet, spiraled through her.

"I want to keep the bargain going," he clarified, "for the summer."

"You want me to take over your rehabilitation, or what's left of it?"

"That's part of it."

"What's the rest? The catch?"

Jake reached out for the end of her ponytail, twirling the ends of her hair around his fingers. "I also want you." His voice deepened to a husky murmur.

Brianne had no doubt he wasn't referring to plain old physical therapy. She kept her eyes trained on his face and attempted to ignore the delicious tugging at her scalp that had an erotic effect on the rest of her body. As did his words. She already knew her response to him, knew each time they came together, no matter how platonic or professional the intent, the chemistry exploded into something much more. She remained quiet, unwilling to tip her hand, to reveal her thoughts or feelings until he'd laid out his meaning before her.

"I'd like to come to an understanding." One side of his mouth lifted in a sexy yet endearingly hesitant grin.

One she knew didn't bode well for her unsteady emotions and racing heart.

"I am willing to cooperate with you. Completely. Enough for you to feel like you aren't lying to Rina when she checks in—and I can guarantee you she will."

Brianne grinned. "She already has. Earlier to-night."

He clenched his jaw.

"But, don't worry, I didn't let on there were any problems. I wanted to talk to you first."

Relief washed over his expression. "I appreciate that."

She tipped her head to one side. "But you'd obviously like something in return?"

"It's not a *quid pro quo,* Brianne. You can say no, and I'll still give you my full cooperation. It's to both of our benefits for my rehabilitation to go off without a hitch. I just think we have something more to offer each other."

Aware of how he affected her, Brianne believed he was right. "What exactly are you referring to?" Her pulse tripped as she awaited his answer, though a part of her already knew.

"I want to explore this attraction between us. You can't deny it exists." With his hands wrapped in her hair, he brought his fingers to her cheek and stroked slowly, methodically, over her skin. "I know *I* feel it every time we're together. Don't you?"

He leaned closer. Their breaths mingled, and a hint of peppermint reached her nose, a scent she'd never found arousing until now. Her heart hammered out a rapid beat. "You know I do. I'm just not certain it would be a good idea." No matter how much his suggestion appealed to her.

"Why not?"

"We're living together, working together...it can get messy." Painful, she thought.

"Or it can be amazing. Think about it, Brianne. An entire summer that belongs to us alone." His eyes blazed with determined blue fire and his finger slid over her face in a lingering caress. "We've already proven we can't be together without fireworks exploding. All the more reason to indulge."

She swallowed hard, his suggestion so very tempting, but if she agreed she knew it would cost her. She was drawn to this man deeply and if she got involved with him sexually, she feared she'd risk losing her heart. A heart she couldn't give to a man who thrived on risk and danger, whom she could lose to a bullet.

But she wasn't ready to divulge all the heartache and pain her past had caused. To share her fears and insecurities would be taking that step toward connecting with him on more than a physical level, something she couldn't afford. "I'm not in the market for a serious relationship. Once the summer's over and my brother leaves for Stanford, I'm going to move to California with him," she told Jake, settling on the easiest truth, one she figured a man would accept and understand.

At her words, something unreadable flickered in his eyes—whether it was disappointment or surprise, she couldn't tell, and he spoke before she could deliberate further.

"I'm not looking for a serious relationship, either. Seems to me every argument you've got strengthens my argument." Obviously Jake wasn't put off and he couldn't be deterred. His deep eyes bore into hers.

"We want the same things—each other and something short term. And we need each other. I need your professional expertise." He paused. "And I need you and this time we could have together. If you're honest with yourself, you'll admit you need it, too."

Brianne's breath caught in her throat. She couldn't

speak even if she wanted to. He was so dead-on accurate, she couldn't argue. Her newfound freedom courtesy of Rina would begin in the fall. But that freedom was scary because she'd been cocooned by her job and responsibilities for so long, she barely knew how to start a life of her own. A personal life.

So just as he needed her professional expertise, she needed his, in areas both sensual and sexual. He was offering her the opportunity to explore her femininity and everything she'd suppressed all these years.

"You want an affair?" she managed to ask, exposing her deepest desire and deepest fear.

"Ideally, yes."

Her stomach twisted with a burning need to agree. After all, she was leaving in September, and they'd be together for the summer. Nothing was stopping her from grabbing this short span of time. Except that everything inside her shouted this man was potentially dangerous to both her peace of mind and her heart.

"I promise you no matter how much *I* want, I'll go slow." His finger stroked her cheek. Soft and sensual, he ignited her skin with a light caress. "I'll go easy." His touch feathered lightly down her neck and teased beneath the *V* of her spandex top. "Seductively," he murmured at last. "And I promise you'll enjoy."

She had no doubt he'd keep his word. Brianne had indulged in past affairs, knowing they could go nowhere. Yet she'd been so desperate for company, she'd accepted less than she'd wanted from life. But even in the midst of those relationships, brief as they were, no man had made her feel as desirable as Jake did.

He wanted an affair. By its definition, short term. No strings. Safe, if she didn't factor emotion into the equation. "You don't ask for much, do you," she murmured.

"No more than I'm willing to give in return."

"What about our patient-client relationship?" she asked, and Jake recognized the last lingering doubt.

She hadn't rejected him outright, and he exhaled hard. "We're alone, no rules or regulations binding us except the ones we make ourselves."

His fingers still lingered on her shoulder, and he savored the feel of her silken skin, wishing he had the freedom to taste and knowing he was a long way from gaining permission.

"When it comes to therapy, I don't fool around," she said, an attractive flush staining her cheeks. "I mean, I don't play games when it comes to rehabilitation. I take my job seriously."

He nodded. "Okay, then, no fooling around during therapy." Damn, but he hadn't meant to constrain himself that way. "I'll take our workouts seriously," he amended. As she'd said herself, therapy was hands-on and no way could he completely refrain from "fooling around" if she agreed to his suggestion.

Though she needed persuading, he could see she was warming to the idea. She just had to put her inhibitions and professional concerns aside.

"You'll work out?" Those beautiful green eyes assessed his sincerity.

"Diligently. You'll give me your free time in between?"

"I don't have much," she warned him.

"Then, it's a good thing my schedule's a lot more flexible. And even better that we're living under one roof. Are you saying we have a deal?" he asked.

The seconds she hesitated were the longest of his life.

Finally she nodded. "We have a deal."

She extended her hand for an awkward shake, but Jake had no intention of letting her off the hook that easily. He grasped her hand, her flesh a smooth contrast to his more roughened skin. "Then, we need to seal our bargain." He pulled her close, and she came willingly.

Her lips parted and her breath caught in her throat. He knew she was waiting for a kiss and he wanted to oblige her, yet as her lashes fluttered closed, he leaned forward and brushed his lips against her forehead instead. Unexpected tenderness washed over him, alien and welcome at the same time.

But that was just the start. He met her wide-eyed gaze. "Slow and easy, remember?"

Her hand rose to cup his cheek. "What happened to seductively?" she asked.

"I think between the two of us we've got that nailed down, don't you?"

"Mmm." Her voice came out like a purr to his ears and, drawn to her in a way that consumed him, he lowered his mouth to hers.

Her lips were soft, pliant and willing, as he slipped his tongue inside. She tasted uniquely Brianne, feminine and warm. Delicious, he thought, and treated himself to a thorough exploration of the heated depths, eliciting a moan of pleasure from her.

The soft sound was all it took for slow and easy to flare quickly out of control. Desire had been simmering for months, denied by distance and fueled by longing. Neither of them was denying now, and the kiss turned hot. What had been a gentle exploration now became a demanding acknowledgment of need. The powerful thrusting of his tongue mating with hers matched the powerful arousal nudging against his jeans, causing an ache only she could satisfy.

He braced his hands on her shoulders, kneading the muscles with his palms and dipping his fingers beneath the front *V* of her tight top, caressing the soft skin on her chest and teasing her with low dips downward with the pads of his thumbs. Her back arched, lifting her breasts, giving him access should he choose to take it. And he wanted to. But his promise of slow and easy echoed in his head, as did her initial hesitance in agreeing.

She'd given him what he desired. And now that he knew what lay ahead, they had time. His body fought hard against that argument, demanding gratification now, but he didn't want the desire between them to burn out too fast.

Though a little voice in his head questioned whether he'd ever tire of Brianne, Jake pushed the notion aside and focused on her instead. But it was that voice, that dangerous thought, warning him against too much too soon, that gave Jake the strength to break the kiss first.

Still, physical contact with Brianne wasn't something he'd give up willingly, and he kept hold of her shoulders, drinking in her dazed eyes, flushed cheeks and damp, parted lips. "Seductively, like I said." He drew uneven breaths, his labored breathing loud to his ears, evidence of the potent desire alive between them.

She touched a shaking hand to her lips. "I enjoyed."

He couldn't prevent a smile. "I always keep my word."

"I like that quality." She smiled in return.

"We'll be good together, Brianne." He squeezed her shoulders in reassurance.

"Oh, you proved that." She let out a laugh. "But we've got other things just as important between us, remember? And just because you tempt me doesn't mean I won't be tough on you during your workouts."

He wasn't surprised she'd brought them back to business. After the searing kiss, her need to latch on to the familiar was understandable. "I wouldn't expect any different."

She licked her lips, and his gaze followed her enticing and distinct reminder of what had just passed between them. But Jake sensed her action was more a nervous reaction than a deliberately seductive move.

"Good." Without warning she rose. "I think we both need to get some sleep."

She was back in protective mode. He respected this side of her as much as he admired her softer, more vulnerable side. He loved learning all facets of this woman, and she obviously had many.

"As long as you don't change your mind come morning."

"*I* won't." She looked at him, all seriousness, but it was the barest hint of vulnerability in her eyes that reached out to him and made him care more than was prudent.

"Me, neither."

She gave him a hesitant smile before disappearing out the door.

Long after she'd turned in for the night, Jake pondered the wisdom of his bargain, wondering if he'd solved his dilemma or merely complicated his life.

BRIANNE PACED outside Victoria's Secret on Fifth Avenue, wondering what had possessed her to ask Kellie to meet her here, of all places. She shook her head. She knew exactly what possessed her. Jake.

Or rather Jake's bargain. Her rapidly beating heart had warned her she was playing with fire by getting involved with the man on any level other than the professional. His kiss, the effects of which she still felt, had proven her right. And what a kiss it had been. Slow, seductive and persuasive, it had quickly flared into much more. The attraction had been obvious from day one, but she hadn't been prepared for the heat they generated each time they came together. And next time, she felt certain, they wouldn't stop with a kiss.

Warmth still suffused her stomach and a pulsing excitement rippled through her veins and settled between her legs, leaving her empty and wanting. Wanting Jake. She'd put her life on hold for so long, and suddenly things had changed. She'd be embarking on an affair, she thought, amazed. And she was completely unprepared.

Last night, Jake hadn't been thrilled when she'd abruptly turned in for the evening, but Brianne had needed time. Not only had his proposition and her own acceptance caught her off guard, but she'd never felt less attractive than she had in her workout clothes and disheveled hair. She wanted Jake to see her as an attractive woman, and she needed to feel like one, and so she'd promised to begin their…liaison—for want of a better word—tomorrow night instead.

And today, she'd taken her first personal time off in ages to prepare. She'd head on back to work this afternoon, but this morning she'd devote herself to the task. And she'd begin by buying sexy underwear.

Brianne glanced at her watch. Although she could handle shopping on her own, she desired feminine advice and company, and for that Kellie ought to be here any minute. Brianne wiped her hand across her damp forehead. The heat outside was getting to her and, after another glance at her watch, she drew a deep breath and entered the store alone. The distinct scent of lavender drifted around her as she surveyed the racks of lace and silk garments dangling temptingly from plush-looking hangers.

The store was a feast for all the senses, making her wonder why she'd never ventured in here before. The obvious answers were money and time, two things she'd never had in abundance. But she did now, and she took in the selection of garments around her. The beautiful matched sets and vibrant colors put her utilitarian cotton panties to shame. She fingered a violet-colored teddy, cut low, and high, in all the right places. The silk slid between her fingertips, soft and sensual, like Jake's touch. She trembled, realizing just what was in store should she be willing to release *all* her inhibitions.

Slow and easy, he'd said. Seductively. He was letting her know she could set the pace, and here she was taking the plunge. The fire in her cheeks matched the heat outdoors, but she'd come too far to turn back now. When the bells on the door tinkled and her exuberant friend walked inside, Brianne knew her fate had just been sealed. Kellie wouldn't let her back out even if she wanted to. She didn't.

Kellie waved, the silver bracelets on her hand jingling aloud. Kellie was a classic blond beauty with huge, blue eyes, a porcelain complexion and a body only every day in a gym would provide. No matter what she wore, men turned their heads and looked twice. Today she had on black jeans and a white fitted T, held together by a row of hooks up the center. It was time Brianne, too, acted more like a woman who intended to make an impression.

"Getting started without me?" Kellie gave Brianne a brief squeeze hello. "It's only been one night, but the place isn't the same without you."

Brianne grinned. "I can't say I miss the long hours on my feet, but I did miss you, too."

"As if you even gave me a thought, with you and the new guy living under the same roof." Kellie rolled her eyes and laughed, obviously not the least bit offended. "So what'd you find so far?" She spread her arms, gesturing to the undergarments around them.

"I just walked in."

"Okay, then, what's this guy's taste run to? The classic or the kinky?" Kellie shook her head. "Never mind. If he's fallen for you, it's classic."

"Are you calling me boring?" Brianne asked, feigning insult.

Her friend shook her head. "You're gorgeous. You just don't take the time to make the most of it. Maybe this new job will give you more time for yourself."

"That's the idea." The money would pay off her brother's tuition, and when the summer was over, her free hours would belong to her alone. There'd never been a time in her adult life when she'd had the luxury of sitting down, taking a breath and saying, *What do I want to do now?*

"The first rule of thumb is if you wear sexy, you'll feel sexy. So what do you have beneath those jeans?"

"Underwear, of course."

"White, I suppose?" She didn't wait for Brianne to

answer. "High-cut and basic? I won't even ask about the bra." She let out an exaggerated sigh. "Looks like I've got my work cut out for me." She grabbed Brianne's hand. "Come on."

An hour later, Brianne had splurged on the kind of lacy, racy undergarments she had never before given a thought to wearing. She'd even left a set on beneath her clothing when she'd walked out of the store. Practice, she'd decided.

And the idea had worked. With the silk brushing her skin as she walked and the knowledge that she wore sheer, sexy panties and a matching bra, Brianne noticed she *felt* more feminine and attractive. Her stride quickened and she lifted her head, glancing around as she walked. Men met her gaze. One leered, his lascivious stare lingering long enough to make her uncomfortable.

But long after they'd left Bloomingdale's behind— bathing suits and a couple of sexy, on-sale outfits bagged and ready to go—Brianne held her shoulders back a bit more, her confidence boosted. All things she could thank Jake for calling her attention to. Not that she'd tell him. The man's ego was healthy enough. But she had to admit, freedom felt good.

"Have time to grab an iced latte?" Kellie asked.

Brianne's throat was parched from the heat and all the walking they'd done. "Sounds great."

"Good." Kellie nodded approvingly, and they walked in silence the few blocks to the nearest Starbucks. In the doorway, Kellie grabbed Brianne's hand and turned toward her. "Clothing and underwear were the hard part. Now we can sit down and talk about sex."

Brianne started to cough, but instead forced a casual shrug. What the heck? she thought. It had been so long since she'd had any, she could probably use all the advice she could get. Her sexual history was minimal. A lukewarm relationship in college squeezed in between her classes and work, and a couple of other guys who'd given up when they realized her brother and her jobs had to come first—and that was it. None of those men had left a lasting or lingering impression. None had eased the loneliness.

But the idea of sex with Jake aroused every nerve ending in her body. Her nipples puckered beneath the new silk, a warm heaviness settled in the pit of her stomach and desire dampened her panties. Though no one could look and know what she was feeling, *she* knew. The intimate, illicit longings were unfamiliar to a woman used to being consumed with work and worries. Being consumed with Jake was a novelty she intended to enjoy.

She shivered in the air-conditioning, but the tremor had nothing to do with the recycled air. Shaking off the sensation, Brianne placed their order while Kellie found a table by the window where they could look out on the nearly empty streets of New York. As it wasn't yet lunchtime, most smart people were inside, away from the oppressive outdoor temperatures instead of enduring the heat rising off the pavement.

No sooner had Brianne carried the drinks to the table and settled herself into a chair than Kellie pulled a box of condoms out of her purse.

Brianne glanced down and swept them under the table. "What are you doing?"

"Making sure you cover all your bases. I know you've had little time for anything lately since you work all day and night—"

"You manage to fit in plenty of extracurricular activity," Brianne said wryly.

"What can I say? I'm resourceful." Kellie grinned. "Not to mention, I don't work nine-to-five during the day. I'm serious. You can't be too careful these days."

Brianne shook her head. "Of course I know that." She glanced down at the box in her hand, shaking them. "There's a lot of those suckers in there," she muttered.

Her friend glanced at her too innocently over her iced coffee. "So, use them."

Brianne's skin prickled at the thought, a renewed awareness and memories of Jake's kiss and searing touch arousing her all over again. And he was so good at that, she thought, mentally transported back to last night.

"Hello?" Kellie waved a napkin in front of Brianne's face. "I take it you plan to? Use the condoms, I mean."

Brianne blinked, focusing on her friend. "Are you sure you don't want them for yourself?" A smile tugged at her lips.

Kellie laughed. "Don't need them. I've got my own collection at home. They're latex and the best protection on the market. Plus they're made for extra sensitivity and have lubrication. Believe me, you want to give one a shot." She wiggled her eyebrows enticingly.

Brianne glanced out the window, her thoughts on exactly what her friend had alluded to—making love with Jake. "Did I tell you the place where I'm staying has a private rooftop whirlpool?" She took a sip of the frothy, cold drink, hoping to douse the flame of desire.

''No, but wow. You are in for one awesome summer,'' her friend said.

''Mmm.'' One group of people, then another, walked past the window. Apparently lunchtime had come for the working people of New York, Brianne thought idly. But she wasn't paying much attention—her thoughts were on herself and Jake on that rooftop.

Suddenly a figure caught her attention, then just as quickly slipped out of sight behind some people exiting a building across the street. The figure wasn't *too* familiar, since she'd only seen the man once before. It had been this morning, after she'd walked out of Victoria's Secret. He'd been the leering one—the one whose gaze had lingered too long, as if he could see through her clothing to the new underwear she was wearing beneath. She'd brushed it off earlier, but what were the chances of her seeing him twice in one day?

A shudder of uncomfortable awareness and revulsion rippled through her.

''What's wrong?'' Kellie asked, following Brianne's line of vision outside.

''Did you…'' Brianne started to ask her friend, then stopped. What was she going to say? Did you see that guy twice today? And if she had, so what? Victoria's Secret was only a block or two from here. The fact that someone had seen Brianne two times that morning didn't make him someone to watch out for.

She shook her head and laughed. ''Forget it.'' Shadowy figures and fear. Brianne had to admit she rarely suffered from anxiety anymore, but sometimes it appeared in ridiculous ways. Her parents had died in a risky situation, a violent storm, but they'd always indulged in some situation or other that put her nerves on edge. She was so unlike her parents, she'd have thought she was adopted if she didn't know differently.

But she was their child and sometimes, as a result, her anxieties resurfaced. "Free-floating anxiety," an analyst she'd seen at the hospital had explained to her. Amorphous anxiety with no basis in the factual situation going on around her now. So what if she'd seen a man twice? That didn't make him a stalker.

"Are you sure nothing's wrong?"

Brianne nodded. "Absolutely. Now, what were you saying?" Shaking off the feeling completely wasn't easy, but with even breathing and a change of subject, Brianne was able to at least feel some semblance of control over her feelings. And that was enough to steady her.

Kellie shrugged. "I said you'd also mentioned a mirrored exercise room in the penthouse. I think you're set, Brianne. You've got all you need for a darn good summer. All you need to do is let yourself go."

She inhaled deeply. *All you need to do.* As if it were so simple, when she'd been single-mindedly focused on her job and her brother for so long. Buying the sexy garments wasn't the same as actually wearing them. She knew that now. And buying the revealing underwear definitely wasn't the same as having Jake see her in them. She thought of Kellie's words again. *Let yourself go.* Yes, it was time to concentrate on *her* needs for a change.

Her needs and Jake's. *That* was all she needed to do.

SHE'D SEEN HIM, Louis thought. She'd looked into his eyes and known he'd been admiring her. How could he not appreciate a babe who was into sexy duds?

How could he not consider the possibility of screwing such a hot creature—and screwing Lowell at the same time?

Now, *that* he couldn't resist. He took a drag, then ground the butt on the pavement with his heel. He didn't think she'd noticed him when he'd walked past the coffee place, but he'd have to be more careful next time. And there would be a next time. Because Lowell had been snooping around, asking questions again. Louis had known within minutes, something Lowell probably knew would happen.

Cat and mouse, Louis thought. So let the games begin. And those games both started and ended with Brianne Nelson. Detective Lowell's woman...but not for much longer.

# 6

JAKE HADN'T DONE surveillance detail in too long. After an afternoon watching a gourmet shop with nothing to show for his effort, he was stiff and frustrated. The only reason the place remained open and hadn't been closed down for good was the lack of proof that linked the pills to the restaurant. They'd gotten a warrant and searched the place based on the circumstantial evidence at the scene, but they'd come up empty. No surprise there, Jake thought. Ramirez was good, and once those kids ODed, he'd clean out fast. But Jake believed the crook was arrogant enough to resume business later.

In theory, the drugs could have come from anywhere. Nothing connected the recent OD to Ramirez—at least, not yet. They were awaiting the toxicology report.

On his way home, Jake had stopped by Frank's place for a visit. He'd played street hockey with Frank's son and shared coffee with Iris, his wife. When Frank was alive, his time with them always reminded him of his failed marriage and all he'd missed out on—kids, a wife who understood him. Since the shooting, the visits had become an emotional ordeal, and all he felt was guilt.

Tonight Jake looked forward to turning his attention to Brianne. She not only attracted him sexually but she made him feel good, something he needed after the day he'd had. During his surveillance watch, he'd wracked his brain to come up with an idea, a place he and Brianne could go. He wanted to get them out of the apartment and into the real world, but he wanted an outing that would be memorable for Brianne.

After an entire day of thinking, he still was at a loss. She'd be back soon, and he had no idea what kind of evening to suggest. Post-therapy, of course. He'd promised her he'd be on his best behavior, and he meant to keep his word.

He walked across the apartment, Norton by his side. After the daily walks and feedings, Norton had grown to trust him more. He still preferred Brianne, something Jake understood, but he no longer whined for hours on end when left alone with an on-leave detective for company. And Jake, having too much idle time on his hands until Ramirez made a move, had begun to appreciate Norton's silent companionship.

He sat down carefully on his sister's velvet sofa, hoping the denim wouldn't rub off on the off-white material. Rina had said not to worry the last time he'd complained, so he settled himself in more comfortably, crossing one leg over the other, waiting for Brianne.

Need and awareness pulsed through his veins and, impatient, he picked up one of the magazines on his sister's marble table and began flipping through the pages. Photos of New York City at night captured his attention, and his gaze settled upon the article's title, "Sexy City Nights."

Tonight would be that and more, he vowed, the wanting increasing along with the wait. One picture in particular caught his attention: two lovers sharing one ice-cream cone, tongues licking the ice cream but so close that it alluded to more. Looking at the photo, the viewer could easily imagine the conclusion, melded tongues as well as dessert.

The thought of Brianne's sweet mouth, flavored with cool ice cream, her tongue licking the side of the cone slowly and erotically as she lapped up the excess drips... His body grew hard and he shifted in his seat, wondering if ice cream would cool him off.

He must have it bad if a simple magazine piece turned him on. But it wasn't the magazine, Jake knew. It was Brianne. His gaze dropped to the magazine once more, and he turned the page. Same background, new photo, and this time the couple shared more than the ice-cream cone, they shared each other. Tasting ice cream off each other's lips.

Ice cream. Jake flipped the magazine closed, no longer needing to distract himself with vague ideas. Thanks to the "Sexy City Nights" article, Jake now had the solution to the special place he could take Brianne. No doubt desserts in her home were parceled out as scarcely as pizza. But he could change that for her, starting tonight. They could share their own sexy city night.

As if he'd conjured Brianne by thought, the elevator doors slid open and she walked into the apartment, a contradiction in dress and appearance. Her normal hospital scrubs told him she'd been at work, but her arms, laden with packages, indicated she'd also been shopping.

"I can't believe how hot the subway was," she murmured to herself. She allowed the packages to topple onto the floor and let out a huge sigh of relief. Norton woke up from his nap and greeted her with a wagging tail and slobbering tongue. Jake had already grown used to the routine.

"Can I help you get those things to your room?" he asked.

She jumped, obviously startled. "I didn't realize you were here." She scrambled to collect her bags without help.

"Should I be insulted you forgot already? We had plans tonight. Therapy, and then I thought we could go for a walk."

Her face flushed redder than it had been from the heat. "I didn't forget, I just..." She juggled the bags once more and ducked one behind her back. "Let me get myself settled." Without waiting for his response, she darted around him and headed toward her room, the Victoria's Secret bag knocking against her work uniform as she walked.

Jake laughed, but his soft chuckle disappeared quickly as he realized the reason for Brianne's nervous behavior and contemplated what might be in that shopping bag. Victoria's Secret sold women's intimate garments—silk, lace, teddies, all designed to enhance and reveal, to make any normal man drool.

Jake wouldn't swear he was normal, but he was a man. The thought of seeing Brianne in any seductive lingerie was enough to send him over the edge. And the mere possibility that she'd bought new things with him in mind... Well, there wasn't much that would cool him down.

Forty-five minutes later, however, he acknowledged that torturous therapy sure took the edge off. Intense pain shot through his shoulder, making the daily ache feel like a woman's soft touch in comparison. He had been working with a therapist since a couple of weeks after the injury, but Brianne's approach was different, more thorough. She'd been right in saying *some* therapy wouldn't be enough. He needed Brianne if he wanted to return to full mobility.

He needed her for more than just rehabilitation, he acknowledged, as he waited for her return from the kitchen with ice packs to cool down his shoulder. He yearned to know more about this woman, a desire that went beyond the physical.

He'd grown up in a happy family. They'd lacked money for extras, but they hadn't lacked love. His parents had been high school sweethearts, and the love they shared permeated the small apartment they'd lived in. Even their move to Florida hadn't lessened the bond that existed between them and their children. He wondered what Brianne's upbringing had been like.

She said she'd raised her brother after her parents died—but what had her childhood been like before she'd been burdened with responsibility? Had she always been this determined, driven person, or had becoming her brother's guardian changed her from a lighthearted girl to a responsible woman?

Knowing she was leaving at the end of the summer, he told himself, he was free to explore, and indulge in, all facets of her and his desire. There'd be no painful breakup when September came. But a small part of him wondered if such a short span of time would be enough to satisfy him.

He shook the thought off, knowing better than to mull over things he couldn't control. He wasn't in a position to change the arrangement, anyway, since even if Brianne were staying, his life was in such turmoil and flux that he couldn't contemplate anything more than a fling. And she wasn't in the market for something longer or more enduring. He'd had one woman give up on him and bail. No way he'd leave himself open to that again.

He had the summer, Jake thought. Now would have to be enough.

PRIOR TO JAKE'S WORKOUT, Brianne changed out of her hospital scrubs and took the time to clean up, makeup and all. For the first time in ages, she'd looked in the mirror and seen a woman staring back. A woman with thoughts, feelings and needs of her own.

And those needs included Jake. Testing his abilities, lifting his arms, feeling his muscles expand and contract beneath her fingertips had aroused her beyond belief, beyond anything she'd felt before—and in her fevered dreams she'd experienced plenty.

Now she paused when she reached the doorway to the gym, ice in hand, and took a moment to watch Jake as he leaned back in his chair and grimaced when the leather touched his bare shoulder. The play of emotions across his face now and as he'd worked out were honest and strong. She felt bad causing him such intense discomfort and pain, but he'd thank her in the long run.

She bit down on her lower lip. He'd said he had been in therapy, and his ability to move proved him right. She wasn't arrogant or presumptuous but she knew without a doubt she could bring him much further than his old therapist had, if only because he seemed so determined and dedicated. She wondered why he'd led Rina to believe he'd done so much less toward his recuperation, then cautioned herself against getting too involved.

She swallowed a harsh laugh. Who was she kidding? She planned on sleeping with the man. Brianne Nelson didn't indulge in one-night stands that meant nothing. Anything she shared with Jake would be intense and memorable, even if she had to leave him behind when the summer was over.

She wanted to know all about him, and she would find out. Asking questions, getting to know him, wouldn't change how she felt about him. She knew she was in danger of falling hard. But whether she fell or not, she'd just have to exercise the same self-control she had in the past. She'd overcome her anxieties in caring for her brother; she'd put her life and needs second to his. Knowing Jake's kind of life could cause her heartache and pain, she'd just have to walk away when their time together was through. If she kept in mind his occupation and his claim that he wasn't looking for a long-term relationship, she shouldn't have any problem keeping things in perspective. Or so she hoped.

She walked into the room and came up beside Jake. "Here. Let's ice down the shoulder." She placed blue gel packs on his bare skin, swallowing hard, knowing how much discomfort he was in and wishing she had more than her professional expertise to make him better. "This will contract the muscles and ease the pain."

"Ahhh."

She recognized his groan of relief and winced, knowing *she'd* caused him this agony. "So what did you have planned for us after this?"

She hoped the change of subject would help him concentrate on something else, and help her concentrate on something other than Jake. And her undergarments. For their session, she wore spandex Capri pants that provided ease of movement, but the tight material showed off both her legs and her behind for his view, as she'd intended. Beneath the skin-hugging material, she wore sexy underthings, and she felt the combination of silk and lace stretch and glide with every move she made. She'd handpicked the mauve panty and matching bra in tactile lace of delicate flowers. Between the flowers, sheerer lace allowed her skin to show through—a lot of skin.

She wondered what Jake would think and how soon he'd have the chance to think it. Her body trembled with delicious anticipation.

"Hey, I'm the one with ice on my shoulder. Are you cold, too?" he asked.

She forced a grin. "I stuck my hands in the freezer to retrieve that ice, remember?"

He nodded. "Are you too cold for ice cream?"

The simple question seemed to hold a wealth of importance she couldn't understand. She met his blue-eyed gaze, which danced with possibility and...hope? She wondered if she was misinterpreting his expression and tone of voice, but she couldn't help but sense her response was important to him. "I'm never too cold for ice cream. Why?"

"What's your favorite flavor?" he asked.

"Well, I'm embarrassed to admit, I'm not picky. Any flavor will do." At that moment, her stomach began to growl, a reminder she'd only had time to grab half a sandwich from the hospital cafeteria for dinner. "Especially now." She laughed and pressed one hand against her stomach.

"Did you have dinner?" His forehead furrowed with concern.

"A little." She'd been too rushed and too nervous about their time together to consume much. "But ice cream sounds great. What did you have in mind?"

"A place called Peppermint Park on the corner of Sixty-sixth and First. They have a huge assortment, and it comes highly recommended by Rina."

"Yum." She ran her tongue over her lips, noticing his eyes followed the movement. She obviously had the power to attract him, and they'd already made the bargain to act on that attraction. Slow and easy.

Did she have the nerve to move up the timetable? Heaven knows, she desired more than food and conversation with this man. His kisses had been just a prelude. She wanted much more.

He pulled his gaze from her lips, but his jaw clenched and his eyes stayed glued to hers, desire in the molten depths. If he kept looking at her that way, they'd never make it out for dessert. But the whole Peppermint Park thing seemed to mean something to him, and the idea of indulging in the creamy dessert held a long-forgotten appeal.

"You know, ice cream sorta fell into the category of pizza. If we had extra, we bought some, but generally we reserved it for special occasions. Birthdays, Marc's graduations, things like that." She shook her head, suddenly embarrassed. "I'm sorry. I don't mean to make my life sound like some *poor me* tale. Believe me when I tell you, all things considered, we had it good."

He reached over and squeezed her hand. "Nobody in their right mind would feel sorry for you. But I am glad to know I picked right." He cleared his throat, and this time she sensed his embarrassment. "I wanted to take you someplace you'd remember. Someplace special.''

Good thing she had already acknowledged that she could fall hard for him and had barriers up to prevent it. Otherwise his concerned expression and tender, generous gesture would definitely steal her heart. She tried not to listen to the voice in her head laughing hysterically at her pathetic attempt to conceal her growing feelings for Jake Lowell.

JAKE SAT on a wooden bench beneath a huge awning, Brianne by his side and Norton at her feet. She'd insisted on giving him an airing, and while she was at it, Jake taught her how to get Norton to "do business" quickly and efficiently. She was impressed by Norton's abilities and obviously pleased Jake had agreed to take the pooch along.

Seeing how happy he could make Brianne—and his sister's dog, he thought wryly—gave him a warm feeling he hadn't had in far too long. He glanced at Brianne. Vanilla fudge ice cream dripped over the sides of her cone, and her little tongue darted out to catch the remains.

Like the photograph. Two lovers sharing something intimate, something more than just an ice-cream treat. Brianne was unknowingly reenacting the erotic photo. Only, she wasn't an anonymous face. She wasn't just his fantasy. She was *his*. Every night for the long, hot summer. He'd already tasted her, knew how her silken mouth and soft lips responded to his.

His fists clenched at his sides as he restrained from acting on his desire. Not now, not yet. He bit hard into his own chocolate-chip scoop and sugar cone, but the sweet dessert didn't provide the kind of satisfaction he had in mind.

"Can I ask you something?"

Brianne's voice was a welcome intrusion. "Sure."

"Well, it's more of a professional question and it's kind of silly, but I was wondering how you know whether you're being followed." Her cheeks turned pink, and she stared at her cone. "See, I told you it was silly."

She was more uneasy than embarrassed, and Jake knew she'd been serious. Seconds ago, he'd thought nothing could distract him from thoughts of making love to her, but she'd managed. "What makes you ask?"

She shrugged. "I was shopping today and I saw a man looking at me."

"Honey, you're beautiful. Men are going to look."

"Thank you." She blushed again. Her gaze met his and lingered, the electricity between them steady and hot, causing a pulsing throughout his body that he couldn't deny.

"But this guy was different," she said, bringing them back to the issue at hand. "I mean, it felt different. I was on Fifth Avenue and he didn't look like your average guy in a business suit during lunch hour. He had this crewcut and leering gaze. And I saw him again. Well, I thought I did, through the window of a coffee shop. And then I blinked and he was gone. And I thought…" She paused, obviously thinking things through.

The ice cream had begun to melt over the cone and dampen the napkin surrounding it. All erotic thoughts gone for the moment, he eased the ice cream out of her hand and dumped their messy cones into the trash next to the bench. "You thought what?"

"That it was happening again." She began twisting her fingers together, and he stilled the nervous movement by covering her hands with his. She shot him a grateful glance.

"You thought what was happening again?"

"When my parents died, I had a hard time." She shook her head. "Actually, it started before that. My parents weren't what you'd call stay-at-home parents. My dad was a stockbroker and he'd done fairly well in some good markets. He had savings, and since they liked to live on the edge, their money went for extreme sports—hot-air ballooning, bungee jumping, motorcycle trips. Good thing the neighbors liked us because we spent a lot of time sleeping at their homes, and my parents weren't reliable about when they'd return. Sometimes I thought they wouldn't come back at all. That's when it started."

Jake wasn't sure where she was going with her story but he wanted to hear more. This was the insight he craved and he wanted to listen as well as to help. "When what started?" he asked.

"Anxiety attacks. I swear, I was such a nervous kid."

He squeezed her hand tight. "Understandable, I'd think. And you must have overcome it well because I'd never have known if you hadn't told me."

"Well, I was lucky I had a good school psychologist, and when I got older I learned stress management techniques. Things quieted down for a long time, acted up again after the accident. Maybe because they had to. It's amazing what you can accomplish when life forces you to grow up quick."

"What accident?"

She frowned, making him want to touch her face, stroke and smooth out the wrinkled skin and then kiss her puckered lips. But he refrained, knowing he would have time later on. For now, he needed her to continue.

"I told you I raised my brother, right? Because my parents died in a small plane crash. Dad was piloting."

She shivered and Jake winced. "I'm sorry."

"It was their choice. Literally. They went up in a storm, weather even the FAA warned against flying in." She sighed, obviously resigned. "So the panic attacks got worse and I went for some short-term help. I needed to get myself under control so I could take care of Marc. And I did. It's been ages since I've experienced any kind of true anxiety."

"Until today."

"Until today," she agreed.

"Then, maybe we ought to give it some credence?" Jake knew he already was. The prickling feeling on his skin and in his gut was strong and sure. He just couldn't put his finger on what was wrong. Yet.

She let out a huge exhale of air, obviously relieved he believed her. "I doubt it. I think I just needed to get it out in the open to see how ridiculous I was being."

"Feelings are never ridiculous and too often they're grounded in fact."

Huge green eyes met his. "Yes, but in my case, I'm probably overreacting. It's probably related to you."

He could see she wasn't comfortable with the admission. He was confused. "How so?"

She swallowed hard. "I hadn't had an anxiety attack in a while, right? And then I met you and we have this instant attraction, and I discover you're just like them. Next thing you know, *boom*. Another anxiety attack.'' She gnawed on her lower lip as she explained.

"I'm just like who?''

"My parents. They lived for taking risks. And that's what you do on your job, right? Take risks?'' One hand reached out and touched his shoulder.

He felt the impact of her touch, the heat and the need, straight down to his toes, but her reassurance didn't help. He was damn sure he didn't like the comparison. "Difference is, I take certain risks in order to do my job, but I don't take unnecessary ones. And I don't do the job as a way of taking risks. Your parents did it for fun.''

"But you both knowingly, willingly, put yourselves in danger.''

He couldn't deny the obvious so he remained silent. She'd equated him to her parents, two people she obviously loved but who'd let her down in the worst way. He'd just met her and was in this for a summer fling. So why did her analogy bother him so much?

"Look, all I'm trying to say is, thanks for listening to my foolishness. There's a reason I panicked, and now that I talked it out I can put it and his disgusting tattoo behind me.''

"Tattoo?'' Jake's nerve endings went on alert, the reason for his wariness and churning gut all too apparent.

"Yes. I don't know what made me think of it now. The guy was in one of those white tank tops, and he had a crooked arrow on his right arm. Biceps. Here—'' She pointed to her right arm and shivered. "Tattoos always grossed me out.''

"Crooked arrow?'' Jake asked tersely.

She nodded. "Like this—" She drew the shape with her hand.

Revulsion and fury raced through his veins. In light of Brianne's history of well-founded anxiety, he had no intention of mentioning that the insignia on the pills he'd just found matched the tattoo on her stalker's arm—the same tattoo that was on Ramirez's right biceps.

He refused to enlighten her and worry her further. The desire to wrap her in his arms and guard her from harm was great. Brianne was no victim. Yet he needed to protect her both physically and emotionally. If she knew there was possible danger relating to Jake and his job, she might bolt. If she returned to her apartment, she'd be vulnerable to Ramirez and Jake would be unable to keep her safe. But if she remained in the penthouse, she'd be safe and secure, at least in the evenings.

As for daytime, Jake could cover her there as well. First thing in the morning he'd call in a favor and have a detective pal put a tail on her during the day. Thank God, Rina was in Italy, Jake thought. But Frank's family wasn't. Unwilling to take further chances, Jake decided to make sure they were covered as well. The department wouldn't assign men on a hunch—they couldn't afford the manpower. But both Jake and Frank had friends who wouldn't mind doing the job. Meanwhile, Jake would step up his digging into Ramirez's hangouts.

For now, he would placate her. "Plenty of men have tattoos. We'll take your suggestion and forget about it, but if you see him again—"

"I'll report directly to you, Detective." She grinned

and treated him to a salute. "But since I'm probably right, you can consider it forgotten."

A touch of chocolate remained on her lips, daring him to reach out and lick it off with his tongue. Instead, he touched the pad of his finger to her mouth, wiping at the chocolate gently, savoring the soft feel of her lips and taking in the curtain of desire shading her eyes.

"Know what I'd like to do now?"

If her voice hadn't dropped a husky octave, he'd have no idea. But it had, and the desire resonating in her tone renewed the heavy tempo beating inside him.

"What's that?"

She drew a deep breath, and he understood being bold was new to her. "I'd like to go home."

"And do what?" He had promised he'd take it slowly. She needed to set the pace, and Jake needed to hear her say the words that would free him from his hard-won restraint.

"Take me home and make me forget." He didn't pretend to misunderstand her meaning. And though her words came out a soft whisper, he heard them every place inside him where it counted.

His gaze never leaving hers, he pulled her to her feet so he could do as she asked. He would take her home.

BRIANNE KEPT PACE with Jake, her rush to get back as fierce as his. Once she'd unburdened herself and admitted her fears, she saw how ridiculous they were. And once he gave credence to her feelings and didn't dismiss her with a pat on the head, as her parents used to do, Brianne was able to step back and see things clearly, with renewed perspective.

She wasn't being followed. She merely had an over-active imagination, heightened by Jake's proximity, lifestyle and job. And on the off chance that a stranger had been watching her, she now had Jake aware and on her side. The self-protection course the hospital had insisted its employees take after a rash of rapes a few years back had armed her with knowledge and defensive skills. She'd be fine.

She could free her mind and concentrate on how much she wanted Jake. Apparently he felt the same, because his hands didn't leave her body the entire trip back to the apartment. Whether on the small of her back or grasping her hand, he held on to her as they walked, creating a constant state of awareness and a never-ending current of electricity that sparked between them.

Only when they reached the inside of the apartment building did he break the physical connection between them, stepping aside and allowing her to pass by him and enter the private elevator. For the duration of the ride up, nerves and excitement dominated her emotions. She was about to dive into sexual and emotional unknown territory, and the adrenaline rushed through her at lightning speed.

She wondered if *this* was what her parents had felt each time they undertook a new adventure or trip. She'd never understood her mother or father before. But as she walked out of the silent but erotically charged atmosphere of the elevator and entered the penthouse apartment, Brianne came as close as she'd ever been to comprehending the thrill-seekers who'd raised her.

Jake was new and exciting. Just thinking about him energized her mind and stimulated her body in erotic and arousing ways. Yet as much as she enjoyed each and every sensation he invoked, she feared, too, for he had the power to undo the healing she'd accomplished since her parents' death, leaving her raw and exposed to someone who didn't come with a promise of security and had no vision of long-term commitment.

But unlike her parents, who by definition were supposed to be in Brianne's life for the long haul, Jake was just passing through. She knew the facts going in; therefore she couldn't be hurt—right? she asked herself. But no voice answered her with a resounding yes, leaving her to admit she had little faith in her own convictions.

"We're here." Jake's deep voice intruded on her thoughts.

She swallowed hard, lifting her eyes from the carpet and meeting his longing stare. He wanted her. She could see the desire flare in the depths of his gaze, a match for the spiraling need building inside her.

He gestured for her to step into the apartment and she followed, her shoes squeaking on the obviously freshly waxed floor.

"Where to?" he asked before they could descend into awkward silence.

An implicit question, Brianne thought. He was asking her where would she like to make love. As she glanced around, liquid heat pooled low in her abdomen and her heart pounded. Her need for Jake was desperate and all-encompassing, but she wasn't so sure how she felt about her surroundings.

She took in the white furnishings, the cold marble floors and the gleaming chrome and crystal accents around her. The penthouse, which had once seemed like a luxurious haven, suddenly felt cold and stifling—stark, in contrast to the warm man standing by her side. Where in this austere place could she be with Jake yet be herself, she had no idea. Unsure of what to say in answer to his question, she merely shrugged, hoping he had the answer she did not.

"Well, I'm using my sister's room and I'd really prefer not to…well, you know what I mean."

"Oh, I do." She laughed, further explanation on his part unnecessary. "But my room doesn't really feel like mine. It's too…"

"Cold and uncomfortable?" he asked, reading her thoughts.

She was glad he didn't find this apartment homey and relaxing, either. "Exactly."

"I honestly don't know what Rina was thinking. This place is so unlike her." His brow furrowed in confusion, and Brianne found the gesture oddly endearing, so different from the manner of the focused cop who'd answered her questions and deflected her concerns.

"Me, neither. Rina has this bubbling warmth. I envy her that." In Jake's sister, Brianne had seen a freedom of thought and emotion she herself had never had, making her feel almost old in comparison. "But you said her husband liked glitz. Maybe she was making him happy by decorating like this. Maybe it was his presence here that made this place a home for them. And vice versa." She shook her head and laughed uncomfortably. "Ignore me. I don't know why I'm rambling like this."

"Nerves, most likely." He nailed her with his correct assumption and innate understanding. "But you're probably right about Rina and Robert. You're definitely perceptive." His voice suddenly grew low and urgent. "And I can't keep my hands off you for a second longer." Without hesitation, his palms came to rest on her shoulders.

Because his skin was hot, he branded her with his touch. And because he was incredibly male, he made her want more than simple conversation or a burning kiss that ended almost before it began.

"Since my room's out and your room's out, I have another suggestion."

She glanced over his shoulder. "It had better not involve that white couch with the full-length windows behind it." She laughed lightly. "So which room will it be?"

"Our room."

As soon as the words were spoken, what had been a light conversation turned into something deeper, stronger and more compelling. The cresting waves of longing she'd held at bay for so long rose furiously inside her. "The gym?"

He nodded. "Full-length mirrors instead of windows."

Her throat grew parched and she couldn't seem to moisten her dry lips. "Different views."

"From different angles. Are you game?"

She'd come this far and she wanted to go much further. Gathering her courage, she raised herself onto her tiptoes and gave him an answer he couldn't mistake—a scorching kiss on the lips, the kind that told him she was indeed game. For any view, any angle, any*thing* he desired.

# 7

DESPITE HER PROTESTATIONS Brianne had an adventurous spirit, Jake sensed. She continually proved him right. First her trip to Victoria's Secret and now this instigation of a kiss. And what a kiss it was. Her tongue glided over the seam of his lips, then retreated, teasing, tormenting him further. His body was strung tight, had been since he'd laid eyes on the beautiful waitress. Unable to wait another second, he grabbed her hand and led her through the apartment, down the hall and into the gym, kicking the door closed and leaving Norton outside.

The room was the only place in this mausoleum where Jake felt remotely comfortable, the only place he could truly be himself and the only place they'd already marked as theirs. And, for some reason, the place he chose was important to him.

It mattered to her, too, if her bright eyes and warm expression were anything to go by. She snaked her arms around his neck and treated him to a deeper, mind-blowing kiss, this one ripe with passion and infused with need—the same need he felt growing, coming to life inside him. He twisted his hips slowly, deliberately, erotically tantalizing her with his full erection pressing hard and insistent against his jeans. She groaned and arched against him, seeking more relief than he could provide through the barrier of clothing.

Jake wanted nothing between them except bare skin. Her clothes were tight and form-fitting, making it difficult to pull and shift so he could eliminate the impediments and give himself complete access. But once the maneuver was accomplished, his view was incredible, thanks to the mirrors surrounding them and the reflection of light.

"You like?"

A light purple bra with flowered lace exposed more than it covered, and he sucked in a ragged breath. "Sweetheart, there's nothing not to like." He traced the scalloped edging with one fingertip, trailing a path over her delicate skin. "And everything to admire." Cherish, bask in, he thought, lowering his head and replacing his touch with his tongue, tasting her bare flesh.

Her response was a rush of air and a moan of contentment, as he followed a damp path across her heated skin. Her shudder shook him as well. Had he ever before felt the way he did now? Wanted a woman's pleasure more than his own?

Jake knew the answer to both questions, and it scared him. He knew he'd have to deal with it sometime, but, for now, the heavy beat of arousal overrode all thought and emotion.

His hand came to rest beneath her breast, cupping the fullness and allowing him to move from the lacy edging to the nipple peaking in a hard ridge beneath the flowered sheath of material. As he drew the distended tip into his mouth and nipped lightly with his teeth, it hardened even more, and the grip he held on his control nearly shattered.

Apparently, she felt the same because her hands went for the snap on his jeans. He lifted his head and met her gaze, not wanting her to feel as though she had to go faster to please him. "I promised you slow."

"That was before we…came this far." A blush stained her already made-up cheeks.

He grinned. "I never said fast wasn't good, too."

God knows, his body would appreciate it if he picked up the pace, but he needed to tell her a few things first. Not just how much he wanted her, but smaller details, too. Things that would let her know she wasn't just someone he'd screw and forget. She held a special place in his life and his heart, he forced himself to acknowledge, and sleeping with her was the answer to every dream he possessed.

"Do you know I loved watching you while you worked at the café? You had on no makeup, just a thousand-watt smile, and I could have watched you all night." The flush on her cheeks deepened, and he brushed his knuckles over her reddened skin. "You're gorgeous with makeup, but you're one of those special women who doesn't need it to make an impression."

Her eyes lightened in wonder and appreciation. "You're pretty amazing yourself, Jake. Waitressing wasn't exactly a job I looked forward to after working all day, but once you showed up…well, all of a sudden I couldn't wait to start my shift."

"Glad to know the feeling was mutual, sweetheart."

She bit down on her lower lip. "There're lots of mutual feelings flowing between us right now."

"I know exactly what you mean." He stepped closer, allowing her to feel his groin push against her. The desire to remove her clothes was as quick and

furious as the need she inspired. She shed her tight
leggings and revealed a pair of lacy underwear, a com-
plement to the barely-there bra. Remembering how
he'd tasted the material around her nipple, the need to
do the same to the lace panties and feminine secrets
beneath grew like an insatiable hunger deep inside
him.

Before she could reach for his shirt, he dropped to
his knees. "You might want to grab on to something
right now."

"You're naughty," she murmured. But the excited
gleam in her eyes told him she desired everything he
wanted to give and more.

He waited till she reached for the exercise bar running across the mirrored wall and then inched closer
to trace the elastic edge of her underwear with his
tongue. The taste was so decadent, her feminine scent
so erotic, he nearly came without being inside her—
hell, without even being touched, something that
spoke of her incredible power over him.

He snaked a path with his tongue, first following
the boundaries set by her panties and going no farther,
teasing her with delicate strokes. But when her legs
quaked and he felt her lean more strongly against the
wall for support, he grew bolder and slowly lowered
the scrap of silk to her thighs, allowing himself to taste
her dewy essence.

Her shuddering moan was all the encouragement he
needed to dip his tongue into her heat and attempt to
draw from her everything he could, give to her everything he had.

Brianne leaned her shoulder against the hard mirrored wall and opened her eyes for a moment. She
glanced down at Jake, his dark hair in stark contrast

to her white skin, his strong hands holding on to her thighs and his mouth doing miraculous things to her long-deprived body. She knew she'd been alone but hadn't realized how lonely she'd been, how empty she'd felt, until Jake possessed her. His arms holding, his hands caressing and his mouth giving to her in ways she'd never experienced before.

Without warning, delicate licks of his tongue were suddenly replaced by bold strokes that made her feel warm and cherished, yet uncontrollably aroused. Each lap was designed to take her higher, closer, and she held on to the bar for support, trying desperately to control the waves rushing through her at lightning speed. But there was no controlling the inevitable, no controlling Jake.

Passion enveloped her, and as she rolled her head to the side, a long, drawn-out groan escaping her throat, she caught a glimpse in the mirror. She saw in erotic detail Jake on his knees, holding her thighs apart, his head dipped in between, worshiping her body in ways no man had ever cared enough to do before. The sight was all it took to send her over the edge.

She shut her eyes and gave herself up to sensation, to the need he had created. And just as the first wave hit, encompassing her body in shuddering bliss, she felt the slide of him inside her, one finger filling the empty space, his thumb pressing hard and deep on exactly the right spot, increasing the magic and prolonging the explosive climax he'd given to her.

It took a while for the rippling sensations to subside, and when they did, Brianne found Jake standing by her side, staring into her eyes. "I've never, I mean no one's ever..." Her words trailed off.

He grinned. "Then, I'm glad I did."

"Me, too."

A muscle ticked in his jaw and the barely leashed desire in his eyes told her that he'd satisfied her but he was by no means fulfilled.

Strangely, Brianne understood. Although he'd satisfied her in one way, in another she was still aroused, still felt an emptiness only he could fill. She felt free to indulge those yearnings and give back to him at the same time. Thankfully, he didn't argue when she reached out to help pull his shirt up and over his head. Male ego versus male desire. No contest there, Brianne thought wryly.

Nor did he utter a complaint when she splayed her fingers over his chest to savor the feel of his coarser, so-masculine flesh. Emboldened, she unbuttoned his jeans and helped him push them, along with his boxers, down to the floor. He kicked the encumbering clothing aside and stood before her completely and gloriously undressed.

Her gaze fell to his erection, and she sucked in a sharp breath.

"Please say that's an appreciative sound." Jake wanted nothing more than to bury his hard, aching body deep inside her.

Somehow she knew. She held her arms out to him, wearing nothing more than the beginning of a slow grin. "Why don't you come find out?"

He didn't need more of an invitation. He grasped her around the waist and had her pinned to the floor in seconds flat. Her body was lush and warm, comforting in ways he'd only dreamed about. He'd also dreamed about being part of her, and he'd stuck condoms in his denim pocket, just in case. He snagged his pants and rolled to his side to take care of protection, then rose over Brianne once more.

"So what do you think? Am I appreciative?" she purred.

Her husky voice ripped his hard-won composure to shreds, and he slipped his hand between them, discovering the moist place between her legs and finding it as welcoming as the woman herself. "I think you're ready for me."

"I think you're right." She spread her legs wide, giving him complete access and utter trust.

He swallowed hard, wondering what he'd done to deserve such an incredible gift, and pushed from his mind the fact that it wouldn't last. He couldn't think beyond now, not when he had a job to do and an uncertain future. If they weren't meant to be, he meant to savor now.

His body was hard and near bursting as he lifted himself over her. "Bend your knees, sweetheart."

She did as he asked and he helped, spreading her thighs. He touched her moist heat with the tip of his penis and she let out a breathy moan, a revelation of exactly how he affected her. He ought to know, since she did the same to him.

"Jake, please." She uttered his name in her soft voice.

"Please what?" He needed her to say what she wanted, needed to know he was giving her all she desired.

Her eyes were bright, her cheeks flushed. "Please come inside me."

As she spoke, her pelvis jerked upward, taking him in one more inch, giving him a taste of what heaven would feel like when he finally earned his way there.

He glided the rest of the way, pushing hard, moving deep, and watching the play of emotions cross her beautiful face.

"Come inside you like this—?" He clenched his jaw. He'd entered her but not the way he wanted. Thanks to his shoulder, he couldn't lean over her, couldn't feel her body flush against his as he braced himself with both hands and drove into her. Still he lingered, braced on one arm.

She shook her head. "Like this—" she said, then took those long legs, wrapped them around his back and raised her hips higher, embedding him deeper, so deep he was practically kneeling astride her, and the penetration drew a whimper from Brianne.

"Hey." He forced his eyelids open. "You okay?"

"Amazing." Her eyes opened wide.

Her expression was nothing short of rapturous and held him by the heart, nearly cutting off his breath.

"It's been so long and it was never like—" She cut off her own words with a kiss meant to seduce him into oblivion, and it did.

But it was only the beginning of his trip. She raised her hips, rolled her pelvis beneath him, and when her feminine mound came in direct contact with his abdomen, she let out a cry, part sigh, part moan. Upon hearing her satisfaction expressed uninhibited from those precious lips, the remnants of his control nearly unraveled.

"We need to switch positions before you kill your shoulder," she said softly.

"I think we can manage that." That she thought of his comfort now caused a softening deep inside his heart, the one he'd walled off years ago. In fact, where women were concerned, he pretended his heart didn't exist. But Brianne wasn't just any woman. He'd known that from a mere glimpse. And now she'd proven him right.

Together they attempted a switch in positions that wasn't easy, but they managed. And then she straddled him. One knee on either side of his thighs, she settled herself on top. The moist heat of her body playfully teased his hard, waiting erection as she subtly shifted her hips.

"Brianne," he said in a warning she heeded. No more games, she took him completely. He was cushioned in her body, thrusting upward without thought, easing his hard length out and thrusting back in sync with her movements. He felt every liquid push and pull of the exquisite friction they created. She was tighter than he'd imagined, and she cocooned him in suctioning warmth.

With each successive rotation of her hips and press downward, she took him in deeper, hugging him in velvet heat. Hugging him in her embrace, causing emotion to swell along with his growing need.

His excitement had escalated the minute she took him in and increased each time they moved, but now as she undulated along with him, meeting him thrust for thrust and encouraging him with a circular pumping motion, he surged and grew inside her until his climax beckoned.

He felt her milking him with her body, heard her calling his name, and, as her breathing shallowed, she began to come. And at that moment, Jake let himself go, reaching for completion, driving himself into her one last time, as hard, deep and fast as he could. His world exploded around him in the most consuming orgasm he'd ever experienced, enveloping him in hot, wet heat, rocking his body with seemingly endless, cataclysmic waves.

Reality returned slowly, and with it the realization of how different this experience had been from any other. How different Brianne was.

Jake took short, shallow gulps of air as awareness returned. Brianne collapsed on top of him in silence, her breathing as labored as his. Without warning, she let out a low groan and shifted off him, causing him to wonder if he'd underestimated her so-called adventurous spirit. Making love on the floor probably didn't qualify as a time a girl would never forget—and he was selfish enough to admit he never wanted her to forget him.

Just as he'd never, ever forget her. "We'd better move," he suggested. He shifted his hips, allowing her to slide off him to lie by his side. The cold rush of air on his body was harsh and unwelcome. "But I liked it better with you covering me."

He wrapped one arm around her, and she curled into a ball, cuddling into him. "And here I was thinking you'd have plenty of objections," he said.

"To feeling you inside me?" she asked with a hint of boldness that seemed to startle even her. "Of course not." She let out a laugh.

"I meant objections to the lack of furniture. The lack of…everything." Once again he was struck by how much he cared about what she was feeling.

She turned and stroked his cheek. "There's no lack of anything. There never is with you. In one night you've given me so much."

"Like what?" He was truly curious. Other than great *sex*, a word that was inadequate to describe all they'd shared, Jake wondered what she thought she'd received.

She nestled her head into his shoulder and sighed. "Well, there's the obvious."

He nodded.

"But there's something else. Did you know I've never had a real date before?"

That surprised him. "I thought you'd been in other relationships."

"I was. One or two to alleviate the loneliness when things got too overwhelming. But it was always something I fit into my schedule, something that was rushed and never made me feel any better than I had before. But tonight you took me out on a real, planned date."

"For ice cream. It was no big deal." But Jake lied to himself, he knew. He'd given plenty of thought to where he could take Brianne. He'd wanted someplace memorable, and though he'd thought of the spot because of a sexy picture he'd seen in a magazine, he'd chosen the place because of Brianne. He'd known in his heart not only that she'd appreciate the chance to indulge in a frivolous treat but that she'd remember him favorably because of it.

"It was a very big deal." She wriggled out of his embrace so she could look into his eyes. "And I think you know it."

He damn well did, and he wasn't just thinking about their so-called date. He'd been married and in love once and he'd been in casual relationships before and since. All paled in comparison to what he'd experienced with Brianne, from looks across a room to the most intimate act imaginable. Jake was a cop, a law enforcement officer, and it wasn't in his nature to deny or lie to himself, professionally or personally. And he knew he hadn't had sex tonight—he'd made love with Brianne.

She sighed and seemed to go boneless beside him, her hair tickling his nose and the scent of strawberries lingering in the air. He wrapped his arms around her waist, but his heart pounded fast and furious as he tried to absorb the implication of how much he cared for this woman who was wrong for him in every imaginable way.

For one thing, she intended to move at the end of the summer. He couldn't fault her for wanting to be near the brother she raised and he had no desire to stand in her way by admitting his growing feelings or asking about hers.

And despite the fact that Brianne understood the value of money more than did most people, Jake still feared he couldn't provide her with all she needed, all she might desire.

And even if he could get past the scars of his marriage, there was something Jake could never overcome. Brianne would never accept what he did for a living. Even if she came to believe differently, one day she'd give up on him the same way his wife had. And though he wasn't sure he'd continue being a cop, Jake's joy and his livelihood would always be tied to some kind of law enforcement. It was "reckless" behavior that Brianne couldn't understand. Behavior that she admitted reminded her of the pain she'd struggled to overcome.

Brianne was his fantasy. At his suggestion, they would have a short-term relationship. A summer fling. Yet when he let himself think about losing her, the pain was blinding.

"There's one last thing you did for me," she said, her words muffled against his chest.

"What's that?" He was eager to put these unexpected emotions and thoughts out of his head and enjoy the time they'd agreed upon.

"I asked you to take me home and make me forget all my ridiculous fears. You really know how to satisfy a woman's request." She snuggled closer, and though his body warmed to her touch, his mind rebelled against everything she'd just said.

He'd planned to make her forget, but he hadn't intended to suffer an amnesiac lapse himself. Yet he had. He'd come back to this apartment, made love to his fantasy woman, *fallen so hard,* he'd nearly lost track of all that was important in his life. A mistake that, if repeated, could cost him everything.

Including Brianne.

Louis was aware of Brianne. How or to what extent, Jake hadn't a clue. But thanks to Brianne's relationship with Jake—perceived or otherwise—she'd become a valuable commodity to Ramirez.

It was too late for Jake to protect her by outwardly pretending Brianne meant nothing to him in the hopes that Ramirez would back off. It was also too late to keep Brianne out of his life. Not only did he want what sacred, limited time they could share, but he needed her around to keep her safe. Having her watched wasn't enough. Jake needed to be involved in her life.

But he couldn't level with her. Since he'd become privy to her painful past, there was no way in hell he could let Brianne in on the fact that, thanks to his job, a dangerous criminal was watching her...and probably planned worse.

The irony was glaring. As Jake had anticipated, his personal and professional lives had escalated at the same time. But he hadn't planned for them to become irrevocably intertwined.

A PATHETIC WHINING NOISE woke Brianne. She opened her eyes and blinked hard. The morning sun shone bright, its golden rays basking her face in heated warmth. She found herself snug in her own bed, Jake curled next to her. They'd made love, and the experience had changed her forever. He'd become a part of her, and wherever she went she'd take Jake with her. Inside her heart, if not by her side.

Last night came back to her more clearly. She remembered them walking down the hall to her room. "Better your bedroom than my sister's bedroom palace," he'd said.

She'd already sensed his discomfort with the overly large and formal apartment, and she was glad to see his taste ran to the more mundane, like her own. She mentally kicked herself for caring what they had in common, when their differences were too great to overcome.

The whine sounded once more, and she realized Norton was closed out of the bedroom and probably needed a walk. She rolled over, glanced at the clock and bolted upright in bed. Norton wasn't the only one who needed to get out of the apartment.

"I'm late." She tossed the covers off her and started to rise, hating the air-conditioned chill but having no choice. Jake stopped her, catching her around the waist, and pulled her back into the downy, warm comforter. Back into his arms.

"Where are you running to?" he asked, nuzzling his nose into her cheek.

"Norton needs to go."

"I took him an hour ago. He's fine, just jealous."

And she hadn't felt Jake leave the bed? She must have slept more soundly than she realized. She was certainly more relaxed, more sated… The red lights on the clock caught her eye once more, and she groaned. "I still need to get to work."

"Don't go." His palm came to rest on her stomach, his hand splaying wide, his skin hot and warm against her flesh.

Her pulse leapt and her insides coiled into a tight, tempting knot of desire. "Do you have any idea how many times I've dragged myself out of bed because I couldn't justify staying home?"

"I'll give you justification." He slid his hand downward, his fingers resting on her feminine mound. Slick moisture trickled between her legs, while a pulsing, pounding awareness started slow and grew until it enveloped her.

"Stay home with me, instead." His husky voice echoed in her ear as his arm snaked out and he reached for the phone, dangling it in front of her eyes. "Come on, Brianne. Call in sick."

She wanted to. She yearned desperately to shed the years of automated behavior and the obligatory need to follow a set schedule. She bit down on her lower lip. "I've never called in sick unless I was deathly ill."

"Then, do it this once. Give yourself a well-deserved treat." One finger dipped lower, teasing her with the beginning of the intoxicating waves he was so good at creating.

"People are counting on me," she murmured, but the protest was weak.

"Then, how about a compromise? Call and say you'll be late." With one smooth move, he rolled on top of her, his naked body aligned and all but joining with hers. Though he wasn't putting weight on his shoulder, the position had to be uncomfortable for him. "I'll make it well worth your while."

He grinned, and she couldn't resist the sparkle in his eye, the warmth and temptation of his body or his willingness to put her needs before his own. Minutes later, her phone call was made and work was pushed aside. As she put the phone back in the cradle, she glanced down at her nightstand drawer and remembered the box of condoms Kellie had given her the other day.

Embarrassed but determined, she opened the drawer and pulled out a foil packet. Then turning back to Jake, she allowed the intimacy they'd shared to guide her as she drew a deep breath for courage and positioned herself on top of him once more. Her legs on either side of his waist, her femininity directly over his erection, she slid down against the length of him, teasing him with what could be. He was hot and hard beneath her, his enlarged member pulsing with desire. For her. Feeling him erect against her, she let out an appreciative sigh.

"Damn, but I like this position."

"I can make it even better." She held out the foil packet she'd retrieved earlier, and he snagged it out of her hand.

"'Extra lubrication and increased sensitivity,'" he read, his blue eyes glittering with want.

"Care to try them out? There's an entire box of them."

"Honey, we are definitely speaking the same language."

She hoped so because her entire body was taut with longing. As if he read her mind, he reached out and cupped her breasts. His large hands kneaded her flesh and satisfied a tiny part of the need he'd inspired. But only a part, because her nipples puckered hard and rasped against his coarser palms. He rubbed gently, increasing the friction and her aching need for fulfillment. In response, her hips began to gyrate in circles against his heated skin.

He gestured with a nod to the condom that had fallen beside him on the bed. "Put it on me."

With shaking hands, she tore into the packet and moved back onto his thighs so she could slide the plastic sheath over his erect penis. With one hand she held his extended length while the other worked the condom over him. She felt every velvet inch and hard ridge of masculine steel. Her pulse pounded, not just in her wrist but between her legs, and a matching trickling of moisture followed.

"You're good at this, Brianne."

Swallowing, she met his gaze. Her hand was still wrapped around him, and she knew for certain she wasn't imagining the play of emotions crossing his face as he watched her. A lump formed in her throat.

Never in her limited experience had the act of protection been a part of sex itself, but now, with Jake, it was foreplay of the most intimate kind. The kind that only occurred between two people who cared for one another, Brianne thought, and she shook the overwhelming, impossible thought away. It was too soon.

They were too new. Yet she knew they'd connected with their first glance and she was lying to herself now.

His hands came to rest on her hips, and he lifted her, still watching intently. Inch by smooth, moist inch, she took him inside her, felt him filling the emptiness and becoming a part of her.

And then he began to move, his hips pumping upward, bringing him deeper, harder. She sucked in a breath and held it fast, then repeated the effort, finding that the controlled breathing brought her closer and closer to release. Her pelvis rocked with his, circular motions that became rhythmic, putting pressure on exactly the right spot at the right time. Each rotation took her higher, higher, until everything exploded in a flash of blinding, all-consuming light and sensation.

He'd just rocked her body, and she knew without a doubt he'd also rocked her world.

JAKE SAT UP in bed, physically sated but mentally alert. The shower ran in the other room, and no matter how much he'd like to join Brianne, he couldn't. He'd bought himself some time by convincing her to go to work late—late enough for him to contact private investigator David Mills, an ex-cop, a damn good detective and the only person Jake trusted to keep an eye on Brianne when Jake couldn't be there himself. He'd already taken care of Frank's family by calling in another favor. And he'd warned Frank's wife to be extra careful, something she understood well.

Jake had attempted to get in touch with his detective friend once during the night, but David's wife and partner said he was out cold after a prolonged stakeout. She'd agreed to take on David's current case to free him up to watch Brianne, and Jake didn't mind owing the Millses a big favor. The stakes were high and the reason worth it. While Jake focused on loose ends, he needed someone awake and alert to protect Brianne.

He'd had to keep her occupied until he could arrange for her safety—not that spending the morning in her bed had been a hardship.

If he'd had any second thoughts about his growing feelings, they'd been answered in the seconds he'd watched her sheath him with protection. His heart had filled as he watched her attempt her task with shaking hands while biting down on her lower lip in intense concentration. And when she'd taken him inside her body, he'd lost a part of himself, probably for good.

He shook his head and cursed aloud. ''Focus,'' he muttered, frustrated with himself and his distracted thoughts. The tattoo and the long-awaited Forensics report would give him a solid lead on Ramirez. Now he had to step up the heat and get Louis behind bars. He was relieved to have set up David to watch Brianne's back during the day. Jake would cover the nights himself.

But who would cover *him* when Brianne walked out for good?

# 8

JAKE HAD GOTTEN Brianne out the door, but not without almost succumbing to the urge to make love to her one more time. And he would have if not for her insistence about getting to work. Jake swallowed a groan, knowing that he'd let his heart rule his head and that it couldn't go on. He had to concentrate on his job.

It was a job that he wanted over and done with so he could deal with his future. For now, the job had brought him to a rendezvous with Vickers at the hospital where the overdose victim had been admitted. And the hospital where Brianne worked.

As he walked up the concrete stairs, Jake glanced around at the crowds on the street, but Ramirez was nowhere in sight. Not that he'd expected the slime to jump out of the shadows and announce himself. But it was the guy's damn lurking that was getting to Jake, making him wary and causing him to wonder what Ramirez had in store for Jake—and Brianne.

He glanced at his watch but his empty stomach already told him it was close to lunchtime.

"Make sure you get yourself something to eat in the cafeteria. I damn sure don't want to listen to that grumbling all morning," Vickers muttered.

Jake laughed, then sobered fast as he remembered

why he'd had no time for breakfast. Indulging in more erotic pursuits, he thought wryly.

"Thompson will have my ass if he finds out I brought you with me to question a witness."

Jake shrugged. The lieutenant was the least of his problems. If Jake ran into Brianne now, he'd have a hell of a time explaining why an on-leave cop with a bum shoulder was hanging around waiting to question a witness.

He glanced at Vickers, a brawny, balding man with good instincts but little tact. "What the lieutenant doesn't know won't hurt him," Jake said. Not that he held any illusions. The lieutenant would hear about his visit one way or another. Jake just didn't give a damn.

"At least if I get reamed I'll have the satisfaction of knowing I won't be the only one." Vickers snickered.

They nodded to the uniformed cop watching the woman's hospital room door, knocked, and, once given permission, walked inside. A drawn-looking young girl—she looked too young to be called a woman—lay in a bed, an IV in one arm and a dazed, bleak expression on her face. Black hair fanned the stark white hospital sheets and drew attention to her utterly pale skin. She turned to look at them as they entered but she didn't utter a word.

Jake stepped back and let Vickers, the detective on duty, begin the questioning. Vickers flashed his badge. "Ma'am, we know this is difficult for you but would you mind taking us through what happened two nights ago?"

A lone tear dripped down her cheek. She looked younger than her twenty-two years but not too young to know better. Why the hell was she experimenting with designer drugs? She was pretty, and too damn young to have been so close to death.

"If you don't want to talk here, we can do it at the station after you're released," Vickers said.

"You're an ass," Jake muttered under his breath. He trusted Vickers like a brother, but the man had the delicacy of an elephant.

When she remained silent, Jake stepped forward. "Telling us what you know won't bring your boyfriend back, but it might save someone else."

She visibly swallowed, then turned her head away from them, obviously unwilling to talk.

"Vick, go get me a cup of coffee, will you?" Jake asked. They'd discussed this scenario ahead of time, and Vickers had agreed if she refused to talk to the police, he'd give Jake, the on-leave cop, time alone with her.

He pulled up a chair and dragged it to the side of the bed. "Cops can be pretty intimidating when they walk in and flash their badges, all full of authority and bull."

She rolled her head to the side and faced him.

A start, Jake thought. "I'm a detective but I'm on leave. Name's Jake Lowell but you can call me Jake." He figured he'd just sealed his chance of the lieutenant finding out about this visit. He'd kill him, but if Jake got information it was worth it.

"Hospitals suck, don't they?" When she didn't reply, he merely continued. "I was laid up myself a while back. I was shot."

She blinked and raised her eyes to meet his. "How'd you get shot?" she asked.

Her soft, melodic voice sounded out of place in the drab hospital room and in the face of her dire circumstances. But at least he'd captured her attention. She was listening. "At a stakeout. Probably by the same guy who supplied those pills you took last night. The pills that killed your boyfriend."

She winced, and Jake felt the slice of a knifelike pain in his gut. He knew he was pushing her hard and being cruel, but he hoped that by reminding her of what she'd lost, she'd fight harder to get the guy who'd done this to her. And maybe by aiding in Ramirez's capture, she'd regain some of the self-esteem lost through the other night's indulgence.

"I'm not an addict," she whispered. "Neither is, I mean, was...oh God...neither was Neil. We just wanted to see what the fuss was all about. I never expected—" Her voice caught and her eyes filled once more.

Jake patted her hand. "I understand. Believe me, I see this more times than I want to count. That's why I need you to help me out, Marina. Help me get the guy. All I need to know is what happened last night. How you got the pills. I'll take it from there."

She let out a huge sigh and nodded. Then, slowly at first and then with more trust and courage, she talked. Jake listened carefully. He already knew Ramirez's MO by heart: Ecstasy delivered to college kids with food as the cover.

Louis had started small, supplying the sandwich man going through the dorms at the local schools, then he'd moved on to the popular restaurant and pub frequented by college students seeking to have a beer or two and unwind. And when they requested the right drink of the night, the patron would receive not only their order but drugs slipped in a rolled napkin.

That was why the pill stuck inside the plastic take-out wrap had intrigued Jake. This girl's version of events was a variation of Ramirez's MO. In this case, instead of a college student, they were postgraduate Psych students in summer school who'd decided, like the other college kids, to let loose and forget studying. They went out and picked up a meal from the newest "in" place. In Jake's mind the similarities were great enough that he refused to rule out Ramirez as the supplier.

"So we ended up at The Eclectic Eatery." She sniffed, and since her hospital gown was too short to be of any use, she wiped her eyes on her bare arm.

Jake leaned over, pulled a tissue from the table beside the bed and handed it to her. "Here—" He shrugged uncomfortably. Though Jake loved the investigating part of the job, he could do without interaction with the bereaved. It was difficult under the best of circumstances, and this was particularly tough.

"Thanks." She forced a smile and rubbed at her eyes.

"You're welcome." He smiled back. "So what did you order?"

"I asked for a Greek salad, and Neil, my boyfriend..." She paused to gulp in air. "Neil ordered something he said was called a falafel, which I'd never heard of. He said it was an Israeli specialty, and The Eatery has dishes from every culture. I always thought Neil was an all-American hot dog or hamburger kind of guy but..." She shrugged.

Falafel? Jake shrugged. Apparently he was all American too, because he'd never heard of the foreign dish. "Did Neil ever ask for drugs?"

She shook her head. "I didn't even know he was going to get them. I'd never done any before. But when we got back to the apartment, he pulled them out of the bag. Like this big surprise.'' She averted her gaze, obviously embarrassed.

"Did you ask him how he got the pills?"

She nodded. "He explained it was all in the ordering."

"Greek salad and falafel will get you drugs?" Jake muttered.

"No. Every dish has a different name. Greek salad is called Hellenic Heaven. Hellenic, as in the ancient Greeks, you know?"

Jake didn't know, but he wasn't about to get into a history lesson, either.

"What did Neil order?" he asked.

A smile briefly crossed her face. "Apparently that Israeli dish also had a history-based name. He said he wanted to taste The Promised Land."

"I'll just bet he did," Jake muttered. He had to admit, the place had a good gimmick going.

But if the substance in the pills or the dead man's body was Ecstasy, Ramirez's drug of choice, the cops would close them down in a heartbeat. Hopefully the toxicology answers would come soon.

Without warning, Jake's beeper went off and he glanced down at the number, then rose from his seat. "Thank you for your honesty, Marina. If I have any other questions, I'll be in touch." He'd also make sure she had a good lawyer for the possession charge that was certain to follow and a counselor to ensure this never happened to her again. He squeezed her arm and stepped into the hall.

"Get anything?" Vickers asked.

"Everything. I'll fill you in on the way out. I'll grab a sandwich at the cafeteria, too." He glanced around.

Secure that he'd escaped without being seen by Brianne, Jake punched the elevator button and was lucky to make a fast escape.

BRIANNE'S HANDS had shaken as she'd worked on every client of the day. Even now as she got ready to take a lunch break, her insides were quaking. She wished she could put the reason into words.

She'd known making love with Jake would change her in some way. She just hadn't realized how differently she'd feel afterward. How much she'd want to stay in his arms and forget the rest of the world—her job and his occupation. And for too many fleeting moments this morning, she'd wondered if there was any way for them to make a relationship work.

Before she could go off on another what-if session, someone tapped her on the shoulder. "Hey, ready to get a bite to eat?" Sharon, another physical therapist and Brianne's usual lunch companion, asked.

Shrugging off the memories of Jake for now, she turned to her friend and nodded. "I'm starving."

"Then, let's go."

They walked through a set of double doors and headed down the maze of corridors that made up the hospital, a maze Brianne could navigate in her sleep. But she wasn't surprised they'd had to redirect more than one confused person who'd ended up in the wrong place.

"Did you hear about the commotion last night?" Sharon asked.

"You worked late yesterday? I thought you got off at five."

The pretty blonde shook her head and laughed. "When was the last time either one of us got out on time? The wife of one of my older patients asked me to spend some extra time with him, and they're so sweet, I couldn't say no. So I was here when an emergency overdose case was brought in.''

Brianne shook her head and sighed. Although her job didn't normally bring her near the Emergency Room, she wasn't immune to the stories or gossip. She couldn't work in a New York City hospital and ignore the often sad stories that floated through the halls. ''There are always OD cases coming in at night. What makes this one so special?''

''She's got her own personal bodyguard. A uniformed cop is stationed outside her door, watching who comes in and out. And you know what?'' Sharon leaned closer and whispered. ''I checked him out this morning and he's *gorgeous.*''

Brianne had her fill of gorgeous cops at home, she thought. She didn't need to see any at work.

''What happened to Tony?'' Brianne asked of Sharon's long-term boyfriend.

Her friend shrugged. ''We're taking a break from commitment. Anyway, you've got to see this guy.'' Determined, Sharon grabbed Brianne's elbow and pulled her down a hall.

''The cafeteria's the other way,'' Brianne grumbled, but she knew the faster she checked out the cute cop, the faster Sharon would be satisfied—and Brianne would finally be eating lunch. Since she'd skipped breakfast, she was starving. But the reasons why she'd missed a meal had left her sated in many other ways— ways more important to her than appetite.

She walked with Sharon, and when her friend paused, rather indiscreetly in Brianne's opinion, across the hall from the uniformed cop, Brianne stopped as well.

"Don't you love a man in uniform?" Sharon asked.

Brianne murmured a noncommittal response. Because one glance at the man in blue told her he couldn't hold a candle to Jake. Then again, she hadn't expected him to. Brianne had a hunch that Jake had set the standard by which she'd judge men for the rest of her life.

She turned to Sharon to ask if she'd had enough, when she caught sight of a pair of men standing by the elevator on the far side of the hall. There were many dark-haired men in the world, but only one with that rebel posture and rugged cutoff sweatshirt. Only one who made her heart race, made her blood pound and made her want to lose her clothes and fall into his bed.

And he was a detective who was so attracted to danger that he couldn't stay away. Not even when he was on injury leave. Not even when he'd been shot and wounded and hadn't completely recuperated yet. The disappointment racing through her system was strong as she accepted the truth: he was a man who would always place himself in danger on a daily basis, no matter what his occupational status.

Brianne's pulse began a thready beat and a wave of light-headedness assaulted her, a combination of shock, nerves and anxiety. Real anxiety, the kind she hadn't had in so long, but the kind she'd experienced again upon meeting Jake. She had no doubt she could overcome it; she just hated that she had to.

Jake. Their connection had been intense and emotional from the beginning. What she felt for him was so strong, so consuming, she was afraid to put a name to it. But raising an adolescent had taught her the value of honesty, and the least she could do was be truthful with herself.

Brianne was afraid she was falling in love with the detective. But love was everything about who a person was inside as well as out. Jake's job was an essential part of Jake Lowell, the man. So how could she have such a strong, negative reaction to his career choice?

If she truly loved him, she had to love everything about him. And she didn't love his job. She admired it, and him—but she couldn't accept the circumstances that went with it. She *chose* not to accept it for herself.

She'd spent years forging a safety net for Marc and herself. And Jake, a narcotics cop, was as far from safe as Brianne could possibly get. Any foolish notions she'd held about making a long-term relationship with Jake work sank along with the elevator he'd stepped into.

JAKE AND VICKERS walked out of the building and into the hot, humid New York City air.

"I hate hospitals." Vickers gave a visible shudder.

"Then you're in the wrong profession, my man." A narc spent too many damn hours in hospitals.

"Well, I'm out of here. I've got some paperwork back at the precinct. I'll call you when the toxicology reports are in."

Jake nodded, swallowing around the last of the dry sandwich he'd picked up inside. While Vickers headed back to the precinct, Jake looked around for David. He found the man in his appointed spot, watching Brianne's back from a location outside the hospital. They'd agreed they couldn't cover all entrances and had settled for the one closest to Rehab. Since Jake couldn't have Brianne tailed inside the hospital without her catching on, he had no choice but to trust she was safe in her daily routine.

He stopped near the sidewalk vendor who was selling hot dogs, hot pretzels and drinks from his cart. "I'll take two colas." Jake pulled some folded bills out of his pocket and paid the man, then walked over to David.

Jake handed a can of cola to his friend. "So what's been going on?"

"Looks like your hunch was right. I saw your pal Ramirez taking a morning stroll outside the hospital about half an hour ago. Maybe he figured Brianne would be coming out for lunch."

Although he'd suspected as much, Jake's stomach clenched when he heard the news. "Damn," he muttered.

"Don't worry. He's close but I'm closer."

"Just keep it that way, pal. And remember, I'm trusting you with my life."

"You mean *her* life," David corrected him, but Jake heard the teasing in his friend's tone.

"I never say what I don't mean, so watch her back." Jake meant no insult. He knew David would do his best no matter what, but telling David how strongly Jake felt about Brianne helped him entrust her life to someone other than himself.

He pulled out his cell phone and dialed Vickers. "Do me a favor. Turn around and come back," Jake said without preamble.

He hadn't wanted to let the police in on Ramirez's interest in Brianne, but now he had no choice. He had to get the scum off the street for good, but he'd settle for Vickers keeping him busy while Jake checked out

The Eclectic Eatery. The cops could pick up Ramirez for jaywalking and detain him for a little while. That was all the time Jake needed to do a little experimenting himself. He'd order off The Eclectic Eatery menu and, with a little luck, he'd score drugs. Then they'd be able to nail Ramirez and keep him in custody where he belonged.

Luck had better be on his side, Jake thought. Because if he came up empty and they had to let Ramirez go, Jake would have to tell Brianne he'd put her in danger—he'd have no choice. Without that knowledge, she wouldn't be aware and careful enough to protect herself inside the hospital. On trips to the ladies' room and supply closets, Brianne needed to be alert and on guard.

But he shuddered to think of her reaction. And he hated causing her pain or a return to the old fears she thought she'd put behind her. He knew Brianne was strong. She'd pull herself together enough to get through this. On a personal level, however, being honest with Brianne would mean not just the end of his summer fling, but losing her trust and faith in him, probably for good.

JAKE STEPPED INSIDE the too-quiet penthouse. With the silence surrounding him, he missed his apartment, a place where he could slam his front door shut in pure anger. Goddamn pansy elevator and its easy glide did nothing to alleviate his frustration. Norton slid on his run to greet Jake as he entered the apartment.

Jake scratched the back of his ear, the same way he'd seen Brianne pet the dog. Norton wasn't satisfied and lowered himself to the floor, seeking a longer stretch of attention. No matter how much love and affection Brianne gave him at night, they were both still gone during most of the day. The pooch was obviously starving for affection if he sought it from Jake. He leaned down on his knees, gave the dog the petting he desired and got slobbered on for his trouble.

Before he could unwind and lose the tension of the day, Jake took Norton for a quick walk. Thank goodness, the dog cooperated, and he was back home before he knew it—home to mull over his unsuccessful trip to the gourmet shop where he'd failed to score. Of course, the order that signaled a request for drugs could change weekly or even daily. Jake had known that going in, but he'd still hoped this case would have an easy wrap-up. For Brianne's sake. He dreaded reigniting her anxieties, and now he had no choice.

The only thing he had going for him—*they* had going for them—was this secure building. As angry as Brianne might be, she'd be foolish to leave here and the safety it offered. At least Jake would still have the summer to get back into her good graces, while keeping her safe at the same time.

He walked down the short hall to her room, but the door was open. A quick knock and look inside told him she wasn't there. He headed across the marble floor and toward the gym, but that room was empty, too. He cursed.

"Today's the day for strikeouts," he muttered.

After he couldn't score the pills, he'd called Duke and discovered the Forensics results were in. Duke had met him on the street away from the precinct, where Jake found out that Marina and her boyfriend had ODed on Ecstasy, Ramirez's stock-in-trade. As far as Jake was concerned, the information was one more nail in the scum's coffin. All they had to do now was link the pills to The Eclectic Eatery and link Ramirez to the restaurant.

Jake's gut told him it shouldn't be difficult. He glanced at his watch and the late hour shocked him. How the hell had the night gotten away from him? He'd been so busy trying to figure out a way to link the pills to Ramirez, he hadn't even noticed the time.

But he noticed now. Where the hell was Brianne? According to her weekly schedule, she was over an hour late. Although he reminded himself she'd been late before, that she could have gotten hung up with a patient or stopped by The Sidewalk Café on the way home, this time felt different in his gut. And Jake never ignored his gut.

He reassured himself that she had David watching her back and the PI would have called if there'd been a problem. If he *could* call. The hell with denim and velvet, Jake thought, and flung himself onto the sofa, grabbed for the magazine and forced himself to flip through the pages. But he couldn't force himself to focus, not even on the intensely sexual pictures. Any-place in a photograph that was intended to be dark and sultry, instead reminded him of Ramirez and the pos-sibility that he was lurking in shadows waiting to am-bush Brianne.

More than once Jake reached for the phone, but tell-ing himself he was overreacting, he sat on his hands. David would call, his mind insisted in direct opposi-tion to his gut. Finally, when another half-hour passed, Jake no longer believed his own reassurances. He and David had agreed that if Brianne was running very late, David would get in touch. As far as Jake was concerned, going on two hours was very late.

With his heart pounding, he grabbed the phone and

punched in David's cell phone number, only to hear a series of rings and a voice-mail greeting.

"Damn." Jake didn't kid himself. Ramirez had killed one cop already. He wouldn't worry much about taking out a civilian. The only option left was David's beeper, and Jake shuffled through his wallet for the piece of paper with the number. But a sound stopped his frenzied actions, and he glanced up in time to see the doors slide open and Brianne step inside. In her ugly green scrubs and ragged ponytail, she was the most beautiful woman he'd ever seen, and relief poured through him—sweet and pure and as fast as the blood pumping through his veins.

Common sense told him to keep his hands off her and maintain a level head. Reason dictated he sit her down and explain the situation he'd gotten her into. But his heartbeat drowned out all rational thought. She was here, she was safe and while she was with him, she was his. And right now those were the only things that mattered.

He rose and stepped into her line of vision.

"Hi, Jake." She eyed him warily, making him wonder if he looked as insane with worry as he felt.

He moved closer, his heart thudding, his need so great he couldn't control it. Jake ought to know better. Hell, he did know better. But not a damn thing could have stopped him as he reached out and pulled her into his arms.

# 9

"YOU'RE LATE." Jake spoke through clenched teeth while he held Brianne in a hug so tight she wondered if he ever planned to let go.

"I take it you missed me?" She forced into her tone a lightness she didn't feel.

His big hands cupped her face and tilted her head back. "You don't know the half of it."

The intensity in his voice and the harshness of his features startled her and shook the rash decision she'd made earlier to call off the affair. After seeing him outside a victim's hospital room with another detective by his side, she'd realized firsthand the danger he put himself into on a daily basis. She'd come far in the years since her parents' death and she could cope with Jake's job—*if* she decided she could handle returning to that kind of uncertain existence. She wasn't sure she'd choose to live that way again.

But faced with reality—cradled in Jake's strong arms, inhaling his masculine scent—her conviction wavered. Even as her more rational self fought against *this*, her emotional, heartfelt needs asserted themselves. She'd known he was a detective prior to going into this affair and yet she'd still agreed. Nothing had changed since then. He was still the man she desired as no other. Why not indulge during the short-term basis they'd agreed upon?

Because her feelings were stronger than the deal they'd made and her heart was at risk, that was why. But nothing seemed to matter when his lips covered hers and he demanded and received entry into her mouth. He devoured her with the same ravaging need that consumed her, his tongue tangling with hers and taking possession. But he gave of himself as well, and Brianne wanted more.

She thrust her hands into his hair, reveling in the way the thick, silky strands slid between her fingers, and she let herself slacken against him, feel his hard body mold to hers. The sensual awareness he effortlessly created rose to life, and a warmth started deep in her belly and pressed downward, creating a heavy, pulsing beat between her legs.

Having already made love with Jake, the desire was deeper and more meaningful than in the past. Her heart beat rapidly, but this time it swelled with emotion, too. Emotion she didn't want to deal with. Not now.

Now she just wanted Jake. To hell with the reality that could tear them apart. This was her summer fantasy and she planned to enjoy it while she could. Perhaps it was the knowledge that *they* could never be, or perhaps it was the danger she'd acknowledged he faced daily, but the rush of want was greater than ever before. She needed him inside her too badly to wait.

Words weren't necessary, not when his eyes spoke of his need and he seemed as eager as she was to get rid of his clothes. With shaking hands and Jake's help, she pulled at his shirt, slowing only to take care with his injured shoulder as she slid his arm out of his sleeve. But once she'd lifted the shirt over his head and tossed it onto the floor, all bets were off. She slid her hands through the light sprinkling of hair on his chest, feeling the flex and pull of muscle beneath her fingertips.

Her palms brushed his hard nipples, and he let out a strangled groan, one that turned her insides to mush and caused a rush of liquid to pool and settle between her legs. As if he knew, he began to tug at her clothes, and soon her hospital uniform lay in a pile at their feet.

His steely gaze raked over her nearly naked body, taking in the sheer, skin-colored bra and panties. Then his hands went to the snap on his jeans. She noted with pleasure that he'd paused to grab a condom from his jeans pocket.

"Honest to God, I haven't carried these things around with me since I was a teenager, but when it comes to you, damn if I'm going to be unprepared."

"I like the way you think."

She liked it even more when she realized his hands shook as well. Within moments she found herself facing his nude body. She swallowed hard and glanced down, noting he'd shed his boxers along with his pants. He was erect, aroused and magnificently male. And he was hers—at least for the summer.

That was the thought that did her in. He extended his hands just as she came into his arms.

"I wish I could lift you up and feel you inside me." He whispered the hot and needy words in her ear.

"Me, too." She glanced behind him, hoping a chair had manufactured itself, but all she saw was Rina's all-white furniture and crystal accessories.

She swallowed a cry of pure frustration as she felt Jake's arm around her waist, urging her to follow him. She did, and soon he was seated on the ledge by the oversize window overlooking the East River, Brianne standing between his strong legs.

The sun was just beginning its lazy descent, and the sky had taken on a pinkish-blue hue. And because the building was the highest around, they had no neighboring buildings blocking their view or intruding on the serenity of their surroundings. Nothing to make her self-conscious or uncomfortable, she thought, and was amazed that, despite how sheltered she'd lived the past few years, being with Jake this way felt natural and right.

As long as she didn't allow ugly reality to intrude, Brianne thought. And she wouldn't, not as long as she had this moment.

He tilted his head back against the clear glass, his fathomless eyes staring into hers. "I want to make love to you with the city behind us," he said in a husky voice.

His tone beckoned not only to the most primal physical part of her, but to her emotions. She trusted this man more than any other, and she needed him as she needed no other.

"I want us where no one can touch us." His heartfelt words secured her feelings and erased any hesitation she might have had. Without instruction, without being asked, Brianne eased herself up so her knees were on either side of Jake's thighs and her femininity was poised over his waiting erection.

She held her balance with only her knees on the ledge and Jake's hands, warm and secure, on her waist. "I feel like I could fall," she said with a shaky laugh.

"Then, by all means, let's anchor you." A naughty

smile lifted the corner of his mouth, and Brianne knew exactly what he meant.

Heart pounding in anticipation, she eased herself up and, with a little help from his nimble fingers, she slid down, his enlarged member penetrating her and filling her.

*Completion.* There was no other word for what she felt, and the truth frightened her. Though she hoped to hide her frantic, overwhelmed emotions, one look into his eyes told her he felt it, too. And Brianne was far from ready to deal with his feelings. She could barely cope with her own.

So she did the only thing she could. She began a steady rocking of her pelvis, shifting her hips and rubbing her feminine mound against his body with a precision that took her to soaring, peaking heights. That was the point—to avoid thinking, to only feel. And she did—his body inside of hers, taking her to a place she'd only imagined.

Her eyelids fluttered open. Big mistake, she realized as she looked into his deepened, darkened stare. Eye contact while making love should have been a distraction, Brianne thought idly. But when everything she saw in Jake's eyes was honest and real, she wasn't distracted. Rather, she was drawn more deeply into the vortex of emotion and desire.

Shook up by the intensity of emotion welling in her throat and the incredible feelings building in her body, she switched her gaze over his shoulder just as he lowered his head and latched on to one of her nipples. He pulled the taut peak into his mouth, alternately grazing with his teeth, then suckling and soothing with his tongue, until she was beyond reason.

Her bucking, shifting body was no longer hers, but

rather something he controlled. And he did it well, his hips pumping upward, meeting every gyrating movement she made and matching it until the most incredible climax beckoned, just out of reach.

He switched his attention to her other breast, but instead of the frenzied need with which he'd started, he picked up a different tempo. Using a slower, circular movement, he laved her entire breast with his tongue. The cool air around them contrasted with his warmer mouth, and with each lap he took of her skin, her nipple tightened and peaked, begging for his attention with a pulling need that found a home between her thighs, where their bodies joined in the most intimate act imaginable. But still he persisted to tease her with slow, methodical strokes of his tongue that had her body writhing and begging for release.

"Open your eyes."

She hadn't realized she'd closed them again, but his deep, husky voice brought her out of her desire-filled haze. She complied, once again meeting his penetrating gaze, and, as she did, he slowed the movements of his lower body until she wanted to cry at the unfairness of his leaving her strung tight and needy.

"I want you to look at me when you come," he said, his voice raw as he explained the answer to her unasked question.

He cupped her full breast in his hand, kneading the plump flesh for a moment. And then, as if she'd told him exactly what she needed, his thumb and forefinger locked onto her nipple and he began to roll and flick at the tender nub just hard enough to bring sensation to life once more. He pumped his hips in an upward, circular motion, never pausing to release his hand or stop the perfect rhythm he'd created. The waves began

in earnest, a steady mounting of desire that encom-
passed her entire being.

And just as she crested, her eyes locked on his and
his climax joined with hers. She came, her body un-
dulating with wave after wave of rapid release. And
as she fell, she caught sight of the skyline behind Jake
and felt as if she were free-falling over the city. Like
her emotions, she was tumbling, body, heart and soul,
without a safety net.

HER BREATHING was rapid and her body still shook
around him, as Jake's awareness returned. He couldn't
breathe any better than Brianne and his body wasn't
on any more solid ground. Neither was his mind, considering he'd avoided facing reality.

He'd needed to tell her she was in danger but, by
the time she'd come home, he'd been so worked up
and worried, he couldn't think let alone form a coherent sentence. One look as she'd walked into the apartment and all he could do was feel. The relief in seeing
her unharmed had been so great, he'd needed to release the fear and prove to himself she was alive. He'd
done that all right. And though he should sit her down
and talk now, he wasn't ready.

As long as they were inside this secure penthouse,
they were safe. And as long as he had some more time
before Brianne looked at him with disappointment and
distrust in her beautiful eyes, he was damn well going
to take it.

He brushed her hair over her shoulder. "You promised me a whirlpool," he whispered in her ear.

Her soft laughter found a home deep in his heart.
"I said if you cooperated I'd *consider* the whirlpool."

"And I've been a very good boy." He didn't add

a word about therapy because the time they'd actually spent working on his shoulder had been minimal and he didn't want her to call him on it just yet. Besides, it hadn't been intentional, and he would let her do all the physical therapy she wanted on his body. Later. Much, much later. When she had no more desire to be in his bed. He shook off that thought as best he could.

A husky purr escaped her throat. "You are *good*, I'll give you that."

She paused to take a nip on his earlobe, and the desire she created rocked him down to his toes. "So the whirlpool it is?" he asked.

"If I don't get out of this position I might never straighten my legs out, and those hot water jets sound awfully good right now." She winced, and he realized how much discomfort she must be in.

He braced his hands on her waist and helped her leverage herself off him and come to a standing position on shaky legs. His body definitely felt the loss, and he intended to make up for it as soon as they hit the whirlpool.

"I can think of many ways to stretch out your legs, and I guarantee you'll feel much better."

"I thought *I* was the physical therapist."

"Just give me a chance to work those muscles of yours. You might be surprised at how proficient I am with my hands."

Her eyes darkened at his completely sexual intent. At least there they were in perfect agreement, Jake thought. He held out his hand and she grasped it, not quite meeting his gaze.

He figured she had issues of her own to work out,

and, considering the upheaval he'd be bringing into her life, he'd give her this time.

He knew it couldn't last.

ON A ROOFTOP high above New York City, Jake led Brianne to the now infamous whirlpool. They'd grabbed towels from the apartment, and he'd taken her via the exclusive penthouse elevator to the private spa on the roof.

The view was incredible. White stars twinkled in the inky night sky and the outline of buildings and lights illuminated the spectacular setting. But the Empire State Building lit up in its red, white and blue glory was the *pièce de résistance*, and stood out from all the more ordinary buildings surrounding them.

Brianne walked to the edge of the roof, and though she kept one hand on the towel around her body, she used the other to grasp the high railing so she could peer out for a better look. "This is almost surreal."

Jake came up behind her. "Pretty amazing, isn't it."

She nodded. "And your sister owns this along with the penthouse? No one else in the building can come up?"

"No one."

She let out a brief whistle. "I guess this is what they mean by wealth."

"Guess so." He propped one hip on a rung of the guardrail. "Nice life if you can get it."

Brianne heard the chill in his voice and was reminded of the only time he'd frozen her out: when she'd verbalized the conclusion that he didn't live in this apartment, that he was a visitor much like herself. She'd wondered then why he'd turned cold, and figured now was as good a time as any to ask.

"Jake?"

"What?" He stared out over the panoramic view of the city, obviously lost in thought.

She tried to come up with a way to formulate the question that wouldn't set him off further, and realized there probably wasn't one. "Why is money such a sensitive issue with you?"

He turned and looked at her. "I suppose when a guy's wife leaves him for what he doesn't have…"

"…he decides to paint all women with the same brush?" She finished the sentence for him, the conclusion not hard to figure out.

"I guess so," he said with a brief nod.

And it hurt, Brianne thought. For so many reasons. The first of which was that she hadn't known he'd been married. The thought of him in love with someone else stabbed her in the heart. Add to that the painful truth—she didn't know much about him at all.

Except how he'd been injured. What it was like to share living space. And the rapture of his body deep inside hers, intimate in a way she'd never felt before. She was wrong. She did know *him*, she just knew too little about his past. And she'd wanted to keep it that way, to avoid the pain of emotional connection.

But it was too late. She'd already entrusted him with personal insight—her parents' death, her difficulty dealing with anxiety and danger, and the frugal way in which she'd been forced to live in order to survive. She'd given to him emotionally despite the risk. It was time she let him talk in return.

But there was another reason his attitude about money and wealth hurt. She'd been open and honest about who and what she was but she'd never once given him the impression she'd taken this job so she could live the good life. In fact, no matter how he looked at it, she was still working two jobs to make ends meet. "It's not like I'm some gold-digging tramp," she muttered.

"No, you are not." He grabbed for her hand.

His low growl and warm touch snapped her out of her internal dialogue and brought her anger to the surface. "Then, why do I feel like you're thinking otherwise?"

"My fault for overreacting." He glanced down as he ran his thumb over her wrist and massaged the pulse point there in an erotic circular motion.

His touch felt wickedly good, but she was more interested in what he had to say. Forcing herself to ignore the sensations traveling from a place as mundane as her wrist to other more private parts, like her breasts, wasn't easy. But she managed, and one second later she was glad she'd remained alert enough to hear his next words.

"And showing my fear."

Her heart leapt in her chest. "Fear of what?" Because Brianne thought she held a monopoly on that particular emotion. Hearing that a big, tough guy like Jake could not only succumb to fear but admit to it was a revelation she couldn't believe.

"Fear of your judging me and finding me lacking, for one thing."

She felt her eyes open wide—along with the heart she'd tried so desperately to keep shut tight. She stepped closer and found herself reaching for his face. A small voice in her head warned her she was treading emotionally deep waters, but she couldn't stop.

His deep blue eyes bore into hers, and she cupped his razor-stubbled cheeks in her palms, the abrading sensation both ticklish and yet subtly arousing against her skin. "How could any woman find *you* lacking?" she asked.

"Do you have any idea what a cop earns?"

A smile worked at the corners of her mouth. "More than I've had left after boarding school bills, I'm sure. But I've never been unhappy. Just overwhelmed, exhausted and cash-poor." She forced a laugh, then sobered quickly. "But if I've learned anything since my parents died, it's that we make our own happiness in life."

"My ex-wife looked to me to make her happy." He shook his head. "Scratch that. She looked to my checkbook. The incredible thing is, she knew all about my lifestyle and what I could and couldn't afford when she married me. She was a teacher, which meant her salary wasn't over the top, either. I really did think we shared the fundamentals. Like the desire for a family."

Brianne's heart ached at the thought of Jake sharing anything with any woman other than herself. *Uh-oh.* "Did you have...kids?" She nearly choked on the word.

He shook his head. "But I wanted them."

Did he still? "What changed?" she asked, quickly denying herself the time to think through the notion of Jake with another woman's baby. The idea was too painful.

"I still don't know. We moved to the suburbs, she met different people, more affluent couples—doctors, lawyers, businessmen." He shrugged. "Then Rina met and married Robert. That couldn't have helped."

"None of that should have changed how she felt about you. None of that should have altered who your wife was inside."

His eyes narrowed, and she could almost see the wheels turning inside his head as he sorted through his past. "Maybe that's it, then. I never really knew who she was inside. I never took the time to find out."

Her pulse picked up rhythm, if only because Brianne knew he'd taken the time to discover who *she* was. Enough to take her on a real date, to bring her ice cream because he thought that had been in short supply in her life. And to give himself, a warm, caring, loving man.

He may not have opened up before but he was doing so now, and she wasn't sure she wanted to contemplate why. He'd started in the permanently off-limits column of her life, and now she wanted to move him over, into the more stable, long-term column. A place he couldn't, wouldn't want to be. He'd made that abundantly clear at the outset.

"Did you love her?" Brianne bit down on her lower lip, wishing she could call back the too-personal, too-revealing words.

"I thought she loved me but it turns out she never fully accepted who I am. What I'll always be. She gave up on me when she realized she couldn't change me."

And that had scarred him badly, Brianne realized, enough to make him wary of other women and of the future. He had good reason. Brianne's reasons for being wary of the future were different but she hadn't fully accepted him and who he was, either. She'd admitted as much to his face. From the beginning, she wished she could change him from someone who loved danger to someone who preferred security and stability.

Is that what she still wanted? Because if she desired

to change him, there was no chance for them or for the future. And a part of Brianne refused to accept that. Confusion twisted inside her.

He reached up and grasped her wrists. She hadn't realized she was still holding on to his face, so natural was the flow of conversation and intimacy between them. And wasn't that intimacy more indicative of what they shared than her dislike of his career? She felt the mental shift occurring slowly and knew she needed time to absorb the implications.

"To answer your question, I suppose I loved the person I married, not the person she became," he said, speaking of his ex-wife. Jake's gaze held Brianne's, full of unspoken meaning. "I realize now that I never loved my ex-wife enough to change and grow with her."

Brianne swallowed hard. "You couldn't have made her happy then, Jake. And vice versa. Money didn't have anything to do with it."

"I suppose you're right."

"I know I am. Look at my life. Money might have given me more free time but I'd still have been a too-young, single woman raising a teenager. All the money in the world wouldn't change that. And it might not have made me happy. I was burdened, yes, but I was also happy." She shrugged, feeling silly revealing herself this way, but not silly enough to stop.

Because this was Jake and he was listening intently, interested in what she had to say and how it related to his past and to them. She drew a deep breath and continued. "Any man in my life would build on the foundation that's already there." The way Jake had. Just the sight of him had lessened her burdens. Being with him lightened her load and made her more complete.

She wasn't ready to take those thoughts to their natural completion so she focused on his past instead. "Sounds like your wife didn't have that foundation."

Admiration filled his eyes along with deeper, more consuming emotion—part desire, but something more. Brianne knew because she felt it, too. "Anyone tell you you're amazing?" he asked.

She shook her head and grinned. "Nope. Care to be the first?"

"Hell, yes." Her first, last, always, Jake thought, and lowered his mouth to hers. The kiss was deep and sweet, but for Jake, just the beginning. "I'm not letting you out of our deal. You owe me a leisurely soak in that whirlpool." He pointed to the bubbling water that was probably as hot as the blood pumping through his veins.

"Then, by all means, let's do it." She inhaled for what he guessed was courage, then took a step back and dropped her towel, letting the fluffy white cotton pool at her feet.

He took one look, and his mouth went dry. She extended her hand, and he followed her to the waiting whirlpool, letting her get in first.

She lowered herself to a sitting position, the bubbling water floating just above her tempting cleavage. When the truth was out, Jake knew what his penance would be—to remember this, remember her and all they could have shared if he hadn't gotten her involved in something guaranteed to bring danger and anxiety into her life, the two things she couldn't and shouldn't ever have to handle again.

Brianne was everything his first wife hadn't been. She was honest, open and real, about herself, her feelings and about her take on life. And in being herself, she'd helped him see his own past more clearly. That was why he intended to savor this night and leave the revelations for morning.

She extended her legs and stretched out, leaning her head back and staring at the night sky. "Good Lord, this is decadent," she murmured.

He settled himself in beside her and let one of the pulsating jets work against his shoulder. "You haven't begun to see decadent. But you will. I promise you that."

"Promises, promises."

"Do you doubt me?" he asked.

"If I say yes, will it get you to move faster?"

His body heated from inside out in a way that had nothing to do with the hot water and everything to do with Brianne. The urgency of their limited time together fueled with his burning desire combined to create a need so strong that it threatened to consume him. "Did I tell you what the beauty of this whirlpool is?"

She shook her head.

"It's got a bench that reclines." He followed his words with his body, moving over to her and easing her down until she rested in the molded seat, her neck and shoulders above the moving bubbles.

She let out a high-pitched laugh. "Water's hitting me from every angle."

He grinned. "Like it?"

She laughed once more, causing him to shake his head in dismay.

"What's wrong?"

"I want you moaning, not giggling. You do realize I'm going to have to do something about that?"

She leaned back against the rounded headrest, her auburn hair floating on the water's surface. Green eyes, as deep as the water's hue, stared back at him, hungry with desire. "I was counting on it."

He leaned over her and his lips came down on hers, the kiss prolonged and sweet. Heaven couldn't feel as good, Jake thought, and slid his tongue inside for a more thorough taste. She let out a soft groan and wrapped her arms around his neck, pulling him on top of her and aligning their bodies in an intimate embrace.

His groin pulsed hard and ready against her bare skin, and her legs slipped open wide, letting him know she was just as ready as he. "One of these days we're going to do this the right way."

"And what would that be?"

"Me on top," he muttered. The lack of strength in his shoulder hadn't slowed him in many things, but making love to Brianne in that particular position had been a luxury denied him so far.

"Work out with me and I'm sure you'll be ready in no time." He couldn't miss the challenging gleam in her eyes. "You know, the whirlpool will heat your shoulder well. We can fit in a session when we finish here."

If she could think about working out, Jake figured he wasn't doing his best to keep her distracted. He extended his hand, and she grasped it and rose to a sitting position. When they finished here, if she was in the mood for anything other than a warm bed and a good night's sleep—tangled in his arms, of course—he'd eat his badge. Besides, she'd need a decent night's rest to deal with tomorrow, he thought, then immediately pushed the troubling future aside.

With a gentle tug, he pulled her between his legs and seated her astride him on the submerged bench.

"Jake?" His name came out a gasp of surprise.

"Relax, honey." He eased one arm around her waist to help her do just that. As she found a comfortable position, her behind pressed gently but insistently against his swelled erection. All his self-restraint went into staying in his seat and not entering her pliant, willing body.

She tensed against him. "You expect me to relax with you inches away from…"

"Yes. Relax and enjoy." He spread his legs, and she went from sitting on top of him to sitting in the *V* of his thighs, his groin hot and hard against the small of her back.

"As if," she muttered.

He chuckled and reached out to play with a few switches on the outside of the tub. Within seconds, the heated seat jets began to bubble away, forcing air upright from the seats into whatever lay directly above them.

From Brianne's shocked gasp, Jake knew exactly where the spurts of air and water had found a home. She wriggled and tried to rise, but he held on tight to her small waist. "Just give it a chance, okay?"

"Okay," Brianne said, but she had no idea how she'd survive it. The pulsating water was hitting her most sensitive, private flesh. And if that weren't enough to drive her mad, she had Jake's erection nudging her back, teasing her with what she couldn't have, no matter how much her body thrummed with delicious, yearning need.

He moved slowly. His arms, no longer locked around her waist to keep her in place, now cradled her, while one palm splayed across her stomach, his fingertips inching downward until he covered her feminine mound with his hand.

She sucked in a startled breath when he dipped one fingertip into her aroused flesh and found the most incredible pressure point in her body. He began a steady stroking motion, each long, slick slide of his finger bringing her higher and higher, until her hips were jerking upward of their own accord, seeking release. Combined with the water jets pulsating against and inside her, her body took over her mind, the need and want so incredible and intense she thought she'd die if the waves stopped—and if they didn't.

Without warning, he raised her higher, and she guessed his intent. Between the two of them, he managed to nudge his penis against her open, needy body. And as he slid her down on top of him, as she took him inside, she felt every hot inch filling her, every ridge of his velvet heat stretching her to accommodate the new but oh-so-incredible angle. Though she'd rather be facing him, looking into his eyes when they made love, ironically this position was intimate, too, more so because of the degree of trust it entailed.

She couldn't see his face or watch his features, and had to believe, to trust, he felt as much as she did.

When his arms wrapped more solidly around her and his hands came up to cup her breasts fully and completely, in what felt more like an expression of possession than lust or sex, Brianne knew that he was engulfed by emotion as well.

And then he began to thrust upward, and it didn't take long for him to lunge to his climax. One last thrust, and she let out a shuddering moan, feeling as if she were flying upward into the night sky.

Heaven only knows how many minutes passed until

Brianne's breathing returned to normal, and eventually she found the strength to climb off him and onto the whirlpool seat so she could cuddle in his waiting arms. She felt so safe there, it was hard to believe she'd spent the afternoon reminding herself of all the reasons he could jeopardize her future. Surely this man couldn't—wouldn't—harm her or her secure life in any way. In truth, she feared she was falling in love with him. Something that wasn't planned and couldn't last.

Her arms snaked tighter around his waist, harsh reality rising to surround her like the bubbles in the whirlpool. They'd been careless—not just with their time together, but by not using protection. Brianne understood why she'd allowed such an intimate act, because of how deeply she both trusted and cared for Jake. And it had been intimate and wondrous, feeling him inside her, no barriers between her body and his.

But it was foolish, anyway. They'd been acting as if they had their entire lives ahead of them instead of one short, blissful summer.

LOUIS SHOVED HIS HANDS into his jeans pockets. Staring up at the tall building, he wondered if the detective and his girlfriend were rocking the walls tonight. For Lowell's sake, Louis hoped so, because it would be the last time. Once any woman had a taste of Louis, she'd never settle for a pig again.

He let out a harsh laugh and lit a cigarette, then shoved the lighter back into his pocket. Yeah, he'd have the redhead and the money that was coming in from his new dealer. The owners of The Eatery had been happy to go into business with him, operating out of both their uptown and downtown restaurants.

Things had been going smoothly, too, until that damn girl and her boyfriend overdosed. Those drugs weren't meant to kill, just to take them a little higher. Now he had Lowell on his back and a witness in the hospital. But if the cops hadn't arrested him by now, they didn't have a damn thing on him.

He shrugged. In the meantime, he was having a blast playing with the detective. Even if Lowell wasn't already uptight and worried about his girlfriend, he would be soon. By tomorrow Lowell would think the only place the beautiful Brianne was safe was his high-rise security building. An illusion Louis couldn't wait to shatter.

# 10

FROM YEARS of training, Brianne had developed an internal alarm that worked like a charm and an uncanny ability to hear her beeper, even in her sleep. Only, she wasn't asleep when the pager went off, she was in the kitchen at seven a.m. pouring a glass of orange juice because she couldn't sleep. Her bag with her beeper was in the living room where she'd dropped it earlier. Before she'd made love with Jake.

Though she'd rather dwell on every erotic memory of their joining, of soaring with New York City in the background, the persistent sound continued. With a sigh, she retrieved her oversize bag and dug through her things for the small black beeper. She was a bit surprised because she wasn't scheduled with a patient until nine a.m.

She checked the number and called the hospital back. Though Brianne normally had patients brought to her at Rehab, occasionally she had an immobile patient that couldn't be moved off the bed but needed strengthening therapy. Mrs. Cohen was one such patient, an elderly woman whom Brianne adored, perhaps because Brianne had no older relatives of her own. The woman had had a skin graft on one leg but still required upper arm workouts so she'd be ready to use her walker when she was allowed out of bed. But why would she need Brianne so early in the morning?

She picked up the phone to find out, but the desk phone on the other end rang endlessly until the hospital's main switchboard picked up once more. The floor nurse could be with a patient or dealing with an emergency. Brianne shrugged and hung up. The page couldn't be a mistake, not at this hour. She'd just toss on her clothes and head out early.

Tiptoeing back into her bedroom so as not to wake Jake, she pulled out a pair of black slacks and a white *V*-necked T-shirt, an acceptable alternative to hospital scrubs, but one she didn't use often because her uniform was quick and easy. She'd lived on the move for as long as she could remember, and she hadn't had time to think about how she looked. She didn't have the time now, either, but the difference was, she cared. Because of the man asleep in her bed.

She made her way to the queen-size mattress and lay down, allowing herself to snuggle beside him for a few precious minutes before leaving for the day. He groaned and pulled her into his arms. He felt so right, so good. She sighed, burrowing her face into his broad chest. He smelled of musk and man, and she'd never felt as safe and protected as she did right now. Ironic, considering he dealt with risk and danger every day.

But *she* didn't deal with that risk or danger. And that enabled her to breathe deeply and enjoy this moment. She shut her eyes and smoothed her hands over the strong planes of his back, memorizing the corded muscle and warm skin, giving herself memories to keep close to her heart while she was gone. Then, with regret, she rolled away. He reached out for her in his sleep, and Brianne felt the beginnings of a smile on her lips. It was easier to leave knowing he'd miss her, too.

She could get used to this too easily, and it could be taken away from her just as fast—by Jake's belief that he didn't want a long-term relationship. Or by a gunman's bullet, Brianne thought with a shudder.

Maybe Mrs. Cohen's page had come at the optimal time, after all. She'd planned on waking up next to him and making love to him again—with protection this time. Their foolishness in the whirlpool couldn't be repeated, nor would she worry unless and until she had to. But making love with Jake in the morning was a luxury she couldn't, shouldn't, make a habit.

No matter how much she was coming to desire otherwise.

JAKE NORMALLY WOKE with the sun, but apparently the late-night activity had worn him out because when he looked up, the clock on the nightstand read 7:48. He felt the warm body heat nestled against him and rolled over, expecting to find Brianne and wanting to bury himself deep inside her again.

Unfortunately, he discovered Norton flush against him instead. "Oh, jeez." He grimaced in disgust. "You are not the warm body I wanted."

The dog didn't move. Jake groaned and pushed himself to an upright position. He still had about fifteen minutes to catch Brianne before she left for work, and regardless of the fact that he wanted to make love to her, he knew he *had* to talk to her instead. Thanks to his stupidity last night, he'd added something else to his list of sins: sex without protection.

Without warning, his revelations to Brianne came back to him. He'd admitted wanting kids. What he'd omitted was that he'd never really been able to envision the family scene with Linda. Things between them had soured too fast. But Jake could too easily imagine it with Brianne. Waking to her warm body in the morning and falling asleep beside her at night. Watching her body change and grow with his child.

Jesus, where had that thought come from? He jumped out of bed, looked for her in the bathroom, then headed for the kitchen. Unfortunately she wasn't there, either. His heart skipped a beat, and the note propped against the coffee machine didn't calm his nerves: "Wish I could have shared the morning coffee with you but I got called to the hospital a little early. Have a cup for me. Brianne."

She'd left him with a full pot of coffee and a burning sensation in his gut. How the hell had he slept through a phone call?

As if on cue, the telephone rang.

He snatched up the receiver. "Brianne?"

"No, David. If she had to be at the hospital early, why the hell didn't you call me? I'd have tailed her or relieved you there."

"She's at work?"

"Yeah, she's there. But I can't do my job if you don't—"

Jake slammed down the phone, cutting David off cold. "Sorry, buddy," he muttered belatedly. And he continued muttering as he pulled on a pair of jeans, a T-shirt and sneakers, grabbed his keys and ran for the door.

This woman would be the death of him. And he wanted to die every morning and every night with her in his arms. But he couldn't do that if she was wandering around, ignorant of the threat Ramirez posed.

He tipped the doorman and asked him to walk Norton, before hailing a cab and heading for Brianne.

He'd put off the truth in favor of selfish need last night, but the morning had come and he had to level with her. Immediately.

BRIANNE RUBBED HER EYES and poured a cup of coffee from the machine in the lounge. She'd gotten here early, and apparently she'd been needed more for emotional support than physical therapy. Mrs. Cohen had become disoriented and had tried to leave her bed. Her family was away, and the name the older woman kept muttering was Brianne's. It was probably because Brianne didn't treat only a patient's body, she treated her mind. She talked to patients while she was working. And she often got the sense that too few people, doctors and family alike, did the same.

She pulled a couple of pink papers out of her pocket, glancing at her messages. One was from her old landlord asking her to come by and pick up her mail—he'd agreed to hold it for her instead of her switching things around for the summer and risking losing important bills and letters. She wondered if there was a reply from the Ranch and shivered. She now viewed the prospect, which had once held great appeal, with increasing uncertainty. Because of Jake.

Brianne took a long, less-than-satisfying sip of the strong, caffeinated brew. She'd need the jolt if she was going to stay awake and on her feet after the night she'd had. And what a night it was—hot, sultry—and she wasn't talking about the weather. That was why contemplating the end of the summer or, worse, the end of her relationship with Jake was so painful. But the alternative was unbelievably confusing. She massaged her aching head once more.

If a summer affair was supposed to be straightforward and easy, why was Brianne so confused about so many things?

She'd always hoped that if she did get the California job, she would enjoy the same kind of warm rapport with the kids that she did with the elderly adults here. But she couldn't know for sure, and Brianne *liked* the geriatric patients she treated. More than she'd admitted to herself. They held a wealth of life history and love, even the cantankerous ones. They counted on her, and she prided herself on knowing she'd never let them down.

And then there was the biggest reason her upcoming move no longer held great appeal. She rubbed at her temples with her right hand. Even if another therapist could take her patients, Jake would still be in New York. Her insides churned, and Brianne understood the reason. She would be across the country, in California with the brother she adored. But he was becoming a man; Marc no longer needed her quite the same way he had when he was younger. She'd called him after leaving Mrs. Cohen and he'd rushed her off the phone; meeting his friends was now more important than talking to his sister. He'd grown up.

Maybe it was time Brianne did the same. Did that mean considering a future in New York, with Jake? She shook her head. What was she thinking? He'd given her no indication he wanted more than a summer fling, and, besides, nothing about their differences had changed. Or had they? Perhaps a better question was, had *she* changed?

"Brianne?" Sharon burst into the room, a yellow, gold and orange bouquet of wildflowers in her hands. "Someone left this on the front desk. It's for you."

Surprised, Brianne took the arrangement and placed it on the table by the old couch.

"Secret admirer?" Sharon asked.

"I don't know." Actually, she did know, and warmth spread through her. She hadn't thought Jake was a flowers kind of guy but apparently she was wrong. She held the knowledge close, having no desire to "share" Jake, her feelings or his gift, by discussing him—even with a friend.

"They are beautiful," Sharon said.

Brianne glanced at the flowers. They were charming and perfect for her. She didn't know what they were called, but she adored the simple arrangement.

The phone in the lounge rang, and Brianne picked it up on the first ring. "Rehab, Brianne Nelson speaking."

"Did you like the gift?" asked a deep male voice with a trace of a foreign accent.

She gripped the phone tighter in her hand. "I think you have the wrong person."

"You said this is Brianne Nelson."

"It is," she said warily, the memory of the man with the tattoo sneaking into her mind. "Who is this?"

"I thought a classy woman like you would have better manners. Don't I deserve a thanks for sending pretty flowers to such a pretty woman?"

"Maybe I'd thank you if I knew who you were." She heard the shaking in her voice and tamped down on her nerves.

But Sharon must have sensed her anxiety; she put a comforting hand on her back.

"No? Well, then you can thank me in person," the stranger said.

"Who *are* you?" Brianne didn't know if she was

dealing with a benign secret admirer or a stalker. Despite her best efforts, trembling turned to shaking, and she eyed the flowers she'd once found lovely with anxious confusion.

"Hang up, Brianne." At the sound of Jake's voice, she whipped around, surprised he'd come to find her here, but not really surprised he'd be around when she needed him.

She didn't question his right to give orders; she just slammed the phone into the cradle and took a step back, away from the floral bouquet.

"Can we have a few minutes alone?" Jake asked.

Brianne glanced at Sharon, who was staring back and forth between Brianne and Jake, obviously unsure of what to make of the situation. Brianne didn't know what to make of it, either.

"It's okay. I need to talk to him," she told her friend.

"You've been holding out on me," Sharon said, a curious yet in-awe expression on her face when she looked at Jake. "If you need anything, I'll be out front."

"Thanks." Brianne glanced at her watch, and though her breathing came in shallow gasps, she somehow managed to go through her schedule in her mind. "Sharon, could you please take my nine-thirty? I'll owe you, I promise."

"Not a problem. You can repay me with information." After another lingering glance at Jake, Sharon walked out of the lounge, leaving the two of them alone.

Jake stood in front of her and squeezed her trembling hands in his. "What happened?" He put an arm around her waist and led her to an old plaid couch.

She'd worked here for so long, yet the couch predated her. It was worn and familiar and gave her a steadying calm she desperately needed. She forced herself to recount her morning, something that helped to calm her nerves. "I got paged on my beeper early."

"And I didn't hear it because…?"

"I was in the kitchen getting a glass of juice and you were still fast asleep. My bag with the pager was still in the living room." And she didn't have to tell him why her purse had never made it into her bedroom last night. The darkening in his gaze told her he remembered everything about last night as vividly as she did.

"Okay, so you were paged. Then what?"

"Is this what they call the third degree, Detective?" she asked lightly. She appreciated not just his concern but his very presence. Sexy razor stubble covered his cheeks, his hair looked as though he'd just tumbled out of bed and he was completely focused on her. He was her fantasy come to life—if the circumstances weren't so unnerving, Brianne thought. At the reminder of that phone call, she shivered and sought to divert her thoughts.

He brushed her hair back from her face, calming her. "This is what they call concern. Now quit stalling and go on."

Brianne had never underestimated his talent or ability as a law enforcement officer, and she saw now that she'd been right. The man was determined, and anyone who needed him would not be let down, but Brianne had no desire to fall into the needy category.

She'd been on her own and strong for too long to let one phone call turn her into a basket case. "I rec-

ognized the extension and called the hospital to see
what they wanted.''

"Is it unusual for you to be paged so early in the
morning?"

She nodded. "Unusual but not unheard of. It wasn't
the Rehab desk, either, so I knew it had to be important. I called back, no one answered, and I figured it
was a real emergency. I found out I was right."

She told him about her elderly patient, and he listened with intense interest. "I told her stories about
Marc and why I became a physical therapist to calm
and distract her."

"Not exactly in your job description." Warm admiration filled his gaze.

She shrugged self-consciously. "What can I say?
I'm a born nurturer."

That she was, Jake thought. And he wouldn't mind
being the recipient of that caring. But with Ramirez
closing in, Jake doubted the fates had that in store.

But hearing her talk about her relationship with her
patients, a smile tilted his lips. "I think those are stories I'd like to hear myself one day." A day when
Brianne wasn't in danger…and if she was speaking to
him again by then.

"I have to warn you, my stories put Mrs. Cohen to
sleep. Though the sedative might have had something
to do with that." She managed a laugh but sobered
quickly, obviously remembering why she was relaying
the story to him.

"I come from sturdier stock than your last patient.
I'm sure I'll manage to stay awake." From his experience questioning witnesses and from his innate understanding of crime victims, he realized that if he let
her continue on a tangent, she would. It was normal

to want to focus on everything *but* the danger she was in.

He would have loved to let her push aside her fears, but he needed her information too badly. He squeezed her hand. "Go on."

She sighed. "Well, after the sedative kicked in and she fell back to sleep, I called Marc. Then I came in here for coffee. Sharon brought me the flowers that were left at the desk. I thought the flowers were from you."

"They were poppies," he said.

She rubbed her hands up and down her arms. "Really? I had no idea. I'm a city girl, remember? I wouldn't know one flower from the next."

"Normally I wouldn't, either." But poppies were associated with narcotics, something any cop would know. The flowers themselves weren't used to make drugs but the sap of an unripe seedpod was the source of heroin, opium, morphine, codeine and more. The flowers had been Ramirez's calling card, something the slime knew Jake would recognize.

Brianne stared at him curiously. "Even a Neanderthal would know roses, but you recognize poppies? I'd never have guessed. The only thing I know about poppies is from *The Wizard of Oz* and the deadly poppy field…"

Her eyes opened wide, and Jake knew the minute she put two and two together, even before she verbalized her thoughts.

"You got shot trying to arrest a drug dealer. I saw you in the hospital yesterday on the same floor as the patient who overdosed."

He inclined his head. Jake hadn't realized she'd seen him yesterday. He let out a groan. He should have known better than to think he'd gotten off easy. With Brianne, nothing was simple.

"Today's delivery of flowers wasn't a coincidence, was it?" she asked, dread showing in her face.

Even though her voice was strong, her cheeks had drained of color. His gut twisted tight. He only hoped she'd continue to hold it together when he revealed the rest, but given her history of anxiety and well-founded fear, he was concerned.

He hated causing her pain and drew a deep breath for courage. "It's no coincidence," he agreed. "And we're talking about the same dealer that shot me."

A visible shudder rippled through her. "And this involves me how?"

She narrowed her eyes, and Jake knew this was it, the time to level. No backpedaling, no ducking out. It was also, he realized, the defining moment in their relationship.

He took her hand in his and looked her in the eye. "You're being targeted by a drug dealer named Louis Ramirez, probably because he's figured out what you mean to me and sees you as a way to get to me." His growing feelings for Brianne had caused exactly what he'd wanted to avoid from the beginning—she'd become a valuable commodity to his enemy.

If anything happened to Brianne, it would kill Jake. Ramirez obviously knew enough to play a cat-and-mouse game—a game Jake didn't appreciate. From the shocked, then angry look on Brianne's face, neither did she.

"I'm in danger because of you?"

He heard the betrayal in her voice, and it struck him like a blow. He nodded. "Indirectly, yes. It looks that way." Technically she was in danger because she'd accepted his sister's offer and moved into the penthouse. But he wouldn't upset her further by clarifying the situation.

From the moment Jake had heard of his sister's meddlesome plan, he'd been filled with dread. He'd just never envisioned Brianne being hurt in any way. If he had, he'd have thrown her out that first day, despite her having accepted Rina's job in good faith. No matter how much she'd tempted him. Jake glanced down at their intertwined hands and felt as if he was viewing his last link to the woman he cared so much about.

"This Ramirez. He has an accent?" she asked through clenched teeth.

Once again, Jake nodded.

"He... He said on the phone that I could thank him for the flowers in person." She yanked her hand free, and Jake felt a loss that went far deeper than the end of physical contact. "How did he know where to find me?"

"He's been watching you." He let his guilty gaze dart away from hers. "For a while now."

"The guy outside the coffee shop?"

"Yes."

She began to clench and unclench her fists, the only outward signs of the anger and betrayal he felt sure were simmering inside her.

"What makes you so sure it's the same guy?"

As a cop, he appreciated her deadly accurate questioning, but as the man who'd violated her trust, he wished she wasn't so quick to put the puzzle together. "The tattoo, for one thing. He's also been seen around the streets outside the hospital."

"Seen by whom?" Brianne asked. But as she

spoke, she began to question more than Ramirez's hidden agenda. She began to question Jake's.

He was certain of too much to be coming into this situation fresh. Since awakening this morning, emotion and confusion had been her constant companions—her stomach rolled, her head ached. And she had a hunch things weren't about to change anytime soon.

He inhaled deeply. "That's where things get complicated." He ran a hand through his hair and stood, then began pacing the floor in front of the couch. "Back when you mentioned you thought you were being followed, I got suspicious."

"But you didn't let on. In fact, you lied." The hurt and the anger she'd been holding back rose to the surface.

"Yes. No." He shook his head in frustration. "I *protected* you. You'd just gotten through telling me you had a well-founded history of anxiety. You equated me to your parents and admitted that when I entered your life, history of danger and all, I'd probably caused all those fears to resurface. I couldn't bring myself to validate your feelings and upset you, or somehow set you off again."

"It's not like I'm some mental patient that needed sheltering! I asked for your professional advice. I didn't ask you to cushion me from the truth." She rose. "I thought I was being followed. I may not have liked it, but I could have dealt with it. I've dealt with a hell of a lot worse."

"That's bull." He shoved his hands into his pockets and met her gaze. "You've dealt with tragedy and come through stronger than you were before. But unless you've dealt with a psychotic like Ramirez, one who'd kill you as easily as he'd blink, you haven't dealt with worse. Not even close.''

At his words, she jerked back, the truth striking her in the heart.

''I'm sorry to scare you, but I'm not sorry for laying out the facts.''

''A little late, but you're right.'' She straightened her shoulders and found the inner strength she knew she possessed. ''I haven't been through worse. This 'psychotic' has been following me. Didn't I deserve the chance to protect myself?'' She pinned him with her glare. She wasn't about to let him off the hook for keeping such a serious secret from her.

He cleared his throat. ''I made sure you were protected.''

''Not very well if those flowers got through,'' she muttered.

''Hospital flowers are delivered all the time.'' He held his hands up in front of him in supplication. ''But I'm not here to argue with you, okay?''

But she'd obviously hurt him, because a flash of pain crossed his handsome face. Still, she couldn't afford to feel sorry for him, not when she had a cop killer sending her flowers and calling her at work. A chill rippled along her spine. ''Protected me how? And don't leave anything out.''

''There wouldn't be any point to that now.''

''But I don't know that for sure, do I? I don't see why you held out on me to begin with.'' She folded her arms across her chest, more to prevent the shaking than as a defense mechanism.

''I've had a detective following you,'' he told her. ''And when he wasn't with you, I was.''

His words shouldn't have shocked her but they did.

She braced her folded hands lower, around her stomach, a way of offering herself comfort, although she found none. A small part of her wondered if Jake's recent interest had more to do with keeping her in his apartment than keeping her in his bed.

He'd been deep inside her body, and they'd made love many times, and so her heart rebelled against the idea. Her mind insisted he'd been drawn to her long before she'd moved into the penthouse and before she'd become a target. But her wounded pride and sense of betrayal still made her question his motives. She didn't want to believe he'd lie, not even in the name of protection.

And she didn't want him to see her as weak. "Okay, so now what, Detective?"

This time he flinched at her formal tone. "This isn't official business for me, Brianne."

"No, you're on leave. But you just can't seem to stay away from the danger. And this time your need for that adrenaline rush brought that danger right to my doorstep."

"*Our* doorstep, or have you forgotten you moved in with me?" he asked through clenched teeth.

He was right. She was blaming him for things that were out of his control. She let out a slow breath. "Okay, so how close are the police to wrapping things up and getting this guy behind bars? Before he gets me, I mean."

Once again he avoided her eyes. "Not very," he admitted, and went on to explain the case as it related to the drug overdose patient in Emergency, including The Eclectic Eatery's probable connection and Jake's inability to score drugs there. "But we haven't been able to link the overdose to the restaurant or Ramirez.''

"Great. So I'm a walking target." The shaking returned along with the unsteady intakes of air until she felt light-headed and dizzy.

He must have sensed her distress because he placed a hand on her arm, but she shrugged off his touch and lowered herself onto the couch. During the course of her personal anxiety therapy, she'd learned intensive breathing that enabled her to create a calm, safe center deep within herself. She ignored Jake and concentrated on steady breathing until the room stopped spinning and she could focus once more.

She opened her eyes to find him staring at her, his blue eyes deep with concern. "Nothing's going to happen to you as long as I'm around. And I'm not leaving your side."

"Just what I wanted, a bodyguard," she said wryly. Especially one who'd slept with her so he would know where she was at night, Brianne thought.

He moved to her side. His masculine scent was overpowering, seducing her with memories of last night. "You know I don't find guarding your body a hardship."

"So you like sex. That hardly makes me feel better right now." But she was lying. Just knowing she had Jake by her side did make her feel much better. More confusion, she thought.

"I'm going to ignore that."

But she didn't miss the hurt in his tone. She knew she was being unreasonably cold toward him, but she couldn't discount the fact that he'd let her wander the streets of New York, unaware that she was being followed by both a drug dealer and a detective he'd hired. She rubbed her hands up and down her arms.

His concerned gaze roamed over her. "You need to be careful, okay? Don't go to the cafeteria or the supply closet or even the bathroom alone. Don't walk anywhere by yourself, do you understand? I'll bring David inside to meet you. He's your bodyguard during the day. He's smart and he's good. What I'm saying is follow the rules and you won't get hurt."

She hugged herself. "And where will you be?"

"Getting Ramirez before he gets you." He turned away.

"Jake, wait." She grabbed on to his arm and held on fast. She didn't want him putting himself in danger at all, but especially not for her.

Because she loved him. *Oh God.*

Love. She should have seen it coming and hadn't. All she'd viewed was mountains of questions and hills of confusion. That hadn't changed. She hadn't a clue how she felt about loving this man who loved danger. She only felt an overwhelming need to protect him from himself.

He pivoted back to her. "What is it?"

"How? How are you going to get him?" she asked, her voice urgent.

"He wants me and he's obviously using you to get to me. If I can't get him for dealing, I'll get him for attempted murder."

Her heart skipped a beat and fear took hold. "Attempted murder of who? You? Who is that going to help?" Brianne asked. Because if anything happened to Jake, it wouldn't help her. But it just might kill her.

"*Attempted,* sweetheart. He's not going to hurt me,

but he is going away. I want him behind bars where he belongs.''

She didn't miss the fiery determination in his gaze or the absolute certainty in his voice. He'd get Ramirez and he didn't care how. Brianne realized she was looking at Jake Lowell, the detective, and the thought of him putting himself on the line scared her more than being in danger herself.

She wanted to believe it was old habits returning. That she was experiencing the same fear she'd felt each time her parents walked out the door on a risky adventure, because she didn't know if they'd come home to her. But in her heart she now knew this was different. Jake was different and so were her emotions and the feelings she had invested in him. She wasn't experiencing a recurrence of old anxieties now. She was scared of losing Jake.

She squeezed his arm tighter. ''You can't make yourself a target. Jake, please. Promise me you won't do that.''

There was regret in his eyes and etched into his handsome features. ''I can't make that kind of promise.''

''Why not? There's an entire police force out there. You're injured and on leave. You aren't in top form. Let someone who's got full strength handle things for you.'' The pleading in her voice reminded her of the little girl she'd once been.

*Mommy, Daddy, please don't go. What if the race car crashes? What if the cord breaks? What if…what if…what if…?* So many variations on the same theme and none of them had made a damn bit of difference. They'd walked out on her, anyway, until one day her worst fears had been realized—they hadn't come back.

From the uncompromising look on Jake's face, he was going to do the same thing.

And, without warning, Brianne realized she had to let him. Because she was no longer that scared little girl, but a woman who'd already undergone the very terror she feared. And she'd survived.

"I'm sorry, but I can't. I have to do this," Jake said.

"I know." Though Brianne didn't like it, she forced herself to admit she understood his reasons. Being a cop was part of who Jake was. He couldn't walk away from a case. And she wouldn't ask him to again.

"You understand?" His shock was tangible. His body jerked backward as if she'd slapped him.

She nodded. "Because I know you. It just couldn't hurt to ask if you'd let someone else handle things." The fact that she understood why he had to do this didn't make it any easier to let him do his job, but she had no choice—just as she had had no choice but to pull herself together and raise Marc.

Until meeting Jake, Brianne had never acknowledged her inner strength, had never had a reason to face or begin to understand herself and the person she'd become. She'd always thought of herself as vulnerable, but she saw now that that was an illusion and she respected herself in a way she hadn't before.

She met Jake's stare. In the blue depths of his eyes, she saw a mixture of awe and uncertainty. He wasn't sure he could trust her faith, and Brianne understood his reasons went beyond her dislike of his job. Jake's ex-wife had bailed out on him—not just on his lack of money, but on *him*. Brianne couldn't do the same.

She leaned over and brushed a kiss over his lips, a gesture meant as a show of faith. He grabbed on to her face and turned the kiss into something deep and meaningful. Or so she chose to believe—because she loved him, she thought once more. And she refused to sit back and let him risk his life to protect her, not without a little help in return.

She lifted her lips from his. "Go do your stuff," she murmured.

He glanced at her, his eyes wide. She'd shocked him again. She wondered if he'd expected her to fall apart; if he believed, because her anxiety had resurfaced, that she couldn't cope at all. It was possible. After all, he'd withheld the truth and hired a PI behind her back. She waited for him to question her, but, without another word, he walked out of the lounge, and a few minutes later returned with her watchdog. David was a burly guy with a baseball cap perched over blond hair and unemotional brown eyes.

She shook his hand and turned away. Though she was grateful for his presence, she was too consumed with the notion of proving to Jake as well as to herself not only that she was strong, but that she was his equal, that she could deal with the Ramirez situation, too. And, in the process, she intended to make sure nothing happened to her fantasy man.

Because when this mess was over, she wanted him alive and well. Not dead on the street. Her stomach churned and dizziness fought its way back, but Brianne, through deep breathing and sheer force of will, managed to stay in control. She'd impressed herself, and a smile fought its way to her lips.

She didn't have a clue how things with Jake would wind up. She still didn't know if she could accept the detective and his lifestyle—for herself and forever.

Whether he even wanted her beyond this summer was also an open question.

The answers would come, Brianne knew, after Ramirez was out of their lives for good.

# 11

EVEN BEFORE Jake left her at the hospital, Brianne realized the only way out of the situation was to face down her fears. Only then would she know if she could handle Jake's kind of life. Only then would she know if she had the courage to approach him and ask for forever.

An hour after Jake's departure, Brianne drew a deep breath and walked into Marina Brown's hospital room. The uniformed cop hadn't given her a hard time, other than to check her hospital badge against hospital records. Mentioning Jake Lowell's name hadn't hurt her cause, either.

"Hello?" Brianne called to the woman curled into a fetal position in the bed.

"Hi." The girl pushed herself up against the white pillows. "Are you another one of the Social Service people?"

Brianne shook her head. "No. I'm..." She swallowed hard. "My name is Brianne Nelson and I need your help."

Brianne figured if she heard Marina's story and discovered how the young woman had gotten drugs from The Eclectic Eatery, perhaps Brianne could attempt to do the same thing herself. It would take some doing, and she'd have to ditch her private investigator, but she'd manage. She'd worked in the hospital for years and knew every back alley and door. She could lose her tail easily. If she could actually get possession of drugs, she could prove the restaurant was the supplier, something Jake said the police had yet to do. After that, the cops could link the restaurant to Ramirez and put him away.

And Brianne would have taken the first step in getting the drug-dealing criminal out of their lives. She didn't think she was smarter than New York's finest, she just needed to take back her life and her future. Ramirez had intentionally and nefariously stolen her freedom, while Jake's behavior—despite the best of intentions—had taken away her control. But between them they had brought back her worst childhood fears. The adult Brianne had to conquer them.

Fifteen minutes later, after an honest exchange with the young woman and a promise to visit tomorrow, Brianne had the general means by which to order drugs from The Eclectic Eatery. She just had no way of knowing which item on the extensive menu was the key. But she'd figure it out.

Brianne rubbed her palms up and down her forearms, then glanced back at the door, behind which the young girl lay with an IV in her arm. She also had a dead boyfriend.

Brianne refused ever to be in that same position. She wouldn't let anything happen to Jake.

"YOU INVOLVED a goddamned civilian," Lieutenant Thompson said in a low growl, eyeing Jake with fury in his eyes.

"Not intentionally, sir." Jake remained standing before his superior, and waited for the smoke to clear and the older man's anger to blow over.

Thompson's face reddened and he kicked a metal garbage pail across the room and into the wall. Obviously the storm wouldn't end anytime soon. Jake didn't blame Thompson for wanting a piece of him. At the moment, he'd like to rip a piece of his own hide as well—for not leveling with Brianne the minute he'd realized Ramirez was tailing her.

But that was hindsight.

Now he acknowledged that Brianne was the strongest woman he knew. She'd overcome her past and raised her brother, and if she'd experienced a resurgence of any anxiety, she knew how to handle it. She'd proven that to him this morning. But at the time he'd realized Ramirez was watching her, Jake hadn't known how she would react; keeping her in the dark had seemed the best means of protection.

But he had another reason for remaining silent— one he didn't like admitting. The truth was that he hadn't wanted to give Brianne the chance to turn him away. She hadn't done it yet but she still might. It was something he wasn't ready to contemplate.

"You questioned a goddamn police witness while officially off duty," Thompson snarled.

"I didn't question her, sir. We had a friendly conversation."

"Friendly, my ass," he muttered. "And your shoulder?"

"Hurts some."

"I don't care how it feels. Is it operational?"

"Close enough." Jake winced as the lieutenant took another shot at the garbage pail. "Did you ever play soccer, Lieutenant?"

The older man scowled. "I don't even want to know the reason you held out on me."

Jake let out a groan and lowered himself into a chair by the desk. He might as well admit to the lieutenant that disillusionment had bit his sorry behind. "Ever since Frank died…" Jake began.

Thompson waved a hand in dismissal. "I said I don't want to know. Not until this is over and Ramirez is behind bars. For now, get your ass into the physician's office and get yourself certified as fit."

Jake nodded, knowing he had no choice if he wanted in on the official end of busting Ramirez.

"Do I know everything now?" the lieutenant asked.

"Yes, sir." Everything but the fact that Brianne was more than his physical therapist. If the lieutenant knew things were personal—and they were damn personal—he'd be even more furious than he already was.

This morning, she'd accepted him for who he was, cop and all. No woman had ever done that for him, not even the one he'd married. Jake hadn't expected the gift from Brianne, not in light of her past, and certainly not after she'd discovered his betrayal. She'd deserved better from him.

"I want to talk to this Brianne Nelson."

Jake started to argue, then shut his mouth. His gut reaction was to protect her, to leave her out of the loop. But he'd played the game that way once before and it had backfired. He hadn't a clue if she planned to walk out on him when this was over, or what he intended to do about it. But he could only deal with the here and now. And Brianne could handle a talk with the lieutenant.

Jake planned to play things straight with her from here on out. "She gets off work at five. I'll bring her down then."

Thompson raised an eyebrow. "I thought you were

her patient, nothing more. I'll have her picked up and brought down here. You don't need to act as her body-guard.''

Jake would guard Brianne's body with his last dying breath, but he wasn't about to fight with Thompson now. Jake ignored the comment and decided to spring his plan on the lieutenant instead. ''Since I've been out asking questions and making his life uncomfortable, Ramirez wants me as much as I want him. I figure we can set me up as a target—''

The phone rang, interrupting him.

''Thompson,'' the lieutenant barked into the phone.

For the first time since Jake had walked into the office and leveled with his boss, the room grew silent. Finally Thompson said, ''Well, I'll be damned.''

He hung up the phone and eyed Jake with a glare that made the hair on the back of his neck prickle. ''What's up?''

''We've got our link between the drugs and The Eatery. Looks like we can shut the place down.''

Jake leaned his hands against the old metal desk and rose. ''Let's go. I'd like to shake the hand of the person who scored.''

''*I'm* going. You're heading for a physical. But don't worry. I'll congratulate your girlfriend for you.'' The lieutenant smirked, telling Jake he'd guessed about his personal relationship with Brianne.

''What?'' The muscles in Jake's back and shoulders tensed and his heart lodged somewhere between his chest and his throat.

''Apparently Brianne Nelson ditched the bodyguard you said was so good and went to The Eclectic Eatery, where she figured out the right request and scored.

Then she called the cops. I don't like a civilian involved, but we're halfway home.''

The lieutenant looked damn pleased they'd connected the restaurant to the goods, but Jake's gut
clenched in pure fear. Brianne had put herself in danger, and if anything had happened to her…if he'd lost
her before he had the chance to tell her he loved her…

He *loved* her. Why the hell hadn't he realized it
sooner?

''Your girlfriend's got talent,'' Thompson said.

''She's not my girlfriend,'' Jake answered automat-
ically, his thoughts still reeling from his realization.
He ignored the lieutenant's disgusted look. Jake never
shared his private life, and despite his self-made promises to the contrary, he sought to protect Brianne now.
Again, when it was obvious she didn't need his protection. Hell, she probably didn't even need him.

But he needed her. Hell, he loved her, he thought
once more. Admitting it to himself wasn't half as hard
as it should have been. The harder part would be admitting it to Brianne…and seeing if she walked anyway.

If she was alive and well. ''Is she…''

''She's fine. Safe and talking to our guys. But if
she's not your girlfriend then why do you look like
you're going to bust a gut unless you get the hell out
of here? I knew there was more to this story. You're
holding out on me again, Lowell. And I don't like it.''

Jake knew when to shut up, so he remained silent.
It was the only hope he had of joining Thompson to
see Brianne.

Thompson's thoughts returned to the case. ''With a
little luck, any employee who's scared enough of hard

time will roll on Ramirez—if they can ID him. And we'll have him behind bars.''

"If he doesn't get Brianne first.'' Jake started for the door.

"Stop!'' Thompson barked.

Jake paused. "Make it quick, Lieutenant. Much as I respect you, I'm out of here.''

"If you want to return to this department—*ever*—you're taking a physical. Now.''

In that instant, Jake's dissatisfaction with his job and his intent for the future crystalized into one thought: *Brianne*. Jake hadn't just been dissatisfied with his career, he'd been dissatisfied with his whole damn empty life.

He didn't have time to think it through now, but he knew his solitary lifestyle and a cop's frustrated duty were the core of his restlessness—summed up with his unpredictable hours and cold meals eaten alone while struggling to nab scum like Ramirez only to have them go free. It had taken Brianne bursting into his life to show him the light.

Jake turned to his superior, a man whom he respected and who'd taught him everything he knew about good police work, procedure, leadership and even friendship. Thompson knew how to balance the two well. Jake would like to sit the older man down and break it to him gently but he didn't have the time.

"Sorry, Lieutenant, but to hell with the physical.'' To hell with the department. The only thing that mattered was Brianne, and when Jake got his hands on her, he was going to kill her. Then he was going to kiss her and make love to her until she was too tired ever to move again.

The older man's eyes narrowed, and he pinned Jake

with his glare. "I'm not having the Ramirez case thrown out again because one of my men put his dick before his brain and screwed up."

Jake didn't take offense. Both men were taking a stand. "Then we're in agreement," Jake said.

The older man slammed his hand down on the desk—a gesture of frustration, but also an expression of understanding because Thompson knew what was coming and didn't like it.

"I'm not one of your men anymore," Jake said.

Thompson swore, but must have known Jake was serious because he didn't argue. "We're out of here. But we're not through, Lowell."

Jake nodded. He owed the older man an explanation, after he got finished with Brianne. Scoring drugs at The Eclectic Eatery! What the hell had she been thinking? He clenched his jaw until his teeth hurt. He didn't give a damn how much he loved her, he'd shake her until her own teeth rattled, he thought, overcome by both fury and fear.

By the time Thompson pulled his car up to the restaurant, now surrounded by cops, Jake was in a sweat. He grabbed for the handle, opening the car door before the sedan reached a stop.

"I suppose you're still going to try to feed me that bull about how she's not your girlfriend?"

Jake ignored the lieutenant. He jumped out of the car and ran to find Brianne.

"It was easier than I'd thought it would be," Brianne told the uniformed cop who was watching her but not really listening. It was his job to guard, not to listen. Besides, she'd already given her story to the detective named Duke, who'd immediately called someone named Lieutenant Thompson. Brianne had a hunch it was only a matter of time before Jake arrived and wanted to strangle her.

She lifted her hair off the back of her neck. The heat was trapped inside the stifling police cruiser where they sat on a side street near The Eclectic Eatery. She'd called the police from a pay phone around the corner—after she'd ordered take-out and discovered she'd actually scored drugs by asking for The Garden of Eden. The description had been simple: a bouquet of mixed greens, tomatoes, bean sprouts and flowers. After her delivery of poppies, the word *bouquet* had jumped out at her and she'd made sure to use it in her order, along with the salad's name. She'd guessed correctly, and in return she'd received a silent nod and, along with her order, little colored pills. She recalled Marina in the hospital bed, and shivered despite the heat.

The police were now waiting for a court-ordered search warrant, and then they'd close down the place for good. Would one of the employees rat out Ramirez? Brianne didn't know but, Lord, she hoped so. The thought of the man's voice and his ability to find her easily put her nerves on edge; she clenched her fists, resting them in her lap.

She still didn't know where she'd gotten the courage to walk into that restaurant in the first place. But somehow, she knew she'd succeed. God knows, she didn't look like a cop, so the restaurant staff shouldn't suspect anything. Still there'd been so many unknowns—was Ramirez already there or was he following her?—yet she'd ditched David, anyway. Not only because she wanted this situation over with, but because she didn't want Jake taking any risks on her behalf. Because she loved him. Her heart still rose to her throat when she admitted it to herself.

And when Brianne loved, she took over. She'd seen herself do it with Marc and now she was doing it with Jake. She put her head in her hands, knowing she still had to face him. In order to prevent him from making himself a target, she'd put herself on the line instead. He'd be furious, she knew, but at least they were a step closer to getting Ramirez out of their lives. After they'd linked Ramirez to the drugs, the case would be over. But for Jake there would be another one after that, then another.

Could Brianne live the rest of her life wondering each day whether he'd walk in the door alive and well? Did he even *want* to walk in her door or was he still tied to the notion of a short-term affair? *Affair.* Such a cold word for such a hot relationship.

A loud thumping noise reverberated through the car, startling her, and Brianne jumped in her seat. She glanced up to see a man's fist pounding on the shatterproof glass window. "It's Lowell. Open up."

Brianne bit down on her lower lip and glanced at the cop in the front seat. Apparently he recognized Jake's voice because he unlocked the doors and stepped out of the car. Minutes later, the front door swung shut, the back door flung open, and Brianne found herself facing Jake.

His face was flushed with anger, his jaw was clenched and his blue eyes were blazing with banked fury, but he remained silent. She winced in anticipation of the tirade she felt sure would come. He lifted his hands and braced her cheeks more strongly than was comfortable but still he said nothing.

She needed to break the tension. "Jake?"

He responded in the least expected way. He sealed his lips over hers, his mouth hard, hot and demanding. He didn't ask, he took, and he pushed his tongue past her barely parted lips in a masterful act of possession. One so strong, she felt the pull both between her legs and deep inside. Sexually, he'd aroused her in an instant, but emotionally he tugged at her heart.

Just as she melted into him, he jerked his head back, breaking the kiss. "I needed to feel you were alive and okay." He ran a shaking hand through his hair.

"I am."

"I know. And now I can throttle you. What the hell were you thinking?" he yelled, the anger she'd expected flooding out.

She blinked hard. He'd never shouted at her before.

"Don't you have anything to say for yourself?" Jake asked.

She shrugged lightly. "I did good, didn't I?"

He lowered his hands from her face, probably to stop himself from squeezing her to death, Brianne thought.

"You could have gotten yourself killed."

Her stomach churned at the thought.

"Why didn't you call me instead of the department?"

She understood his anger and frustration. But she'd entered that store in part to keep Jake out of danger and in part to make sure Ramirez stayed behind bars this time. Calling Jake would have been an emotional reaction, so she'd refrained.

"Because I was afraid Ramirez's lawyer would say any evidence I got was tainted. Is that the right word? You're not on official duty and you have a grudge. I didn't want him to claim entrapment and get off again.'' She shrugged, and when he didn't reply, she continued. "I was protecting you and your case. And afterward, I wanted to call you but the police wouldn't let me. They said they'd handle things from here, put me in this patrol car and—"

His sharp exhale told her he'd accepted her explanation, although he was by no means calmer. "You need to give your statement, and then we're going home," he said tersely.

"I already gave information to an officer."

"Lieutenant Thompson wants to talk to you, and you'll need to give an official statement downtown. Then we're going back to the penthouse and you're not leaving there until Ramirez is behind bars."

"Now *that's* a little extreme, don't you think?"

"You don't want to test me right now, Brianne."

His anger was palpable. So was his fear. He braced one arm on top of the back seat and leaned close. His masculine scent wrapped around her, overpowering her in the confines of the small car.

"You want to do exactly as I say and let me take you home."

Her stomach did an excited flip at his insistent, severe tone. Reaching up, she touched her fingers to his cheek, then let them roam downward until she found the muscle in his jaw and massaged the side of his face. "I'm sorry I scared you," she said softly.

He remained outwardly unaffected by her touch. "Do you have any idea what could have happened to you if Ramirez had gotten a hold of you?"

She shivered. "He didn't."

"He could have."

Neither his tone nor his expression showed any sign

of softening, and her heart pounded in her chest. "Jake…"

Just then, a thunderous voice called his name and pounded on the top of the car. "Lowell, get the hell out here."

"Sounds like someone's not thrilled with you." Brianne tried to see who was out there and couldn't.

"Pretty much how I'm feeling about you right now," Jake muttered.

She cringed when another *thump* sounded on the roof. "Now," the male voice yelled.

She crossed her arms over her chest, bracing her hands around her forearms. "You're being summoned." And none too soon, she thought.

Jake nodded, then jerked open the car door and jumped out, slamming the door closed before she could make an exit of her own.

That was okay, Brianne thought. She could use the time to figure out how to neutralize Jake's fury. Though she felt awful about scaring him, she refused to back down as if she'd done anything wrong. She'd put Jake first, before her fear. If given the choice again, she'd do the exact same thing.

AFTER AN EXHAUSTING couple of hours at the police station, Jake took Brianne home to the penthouse. The cops had confiscated the drugs, more than they'd thought they would get in one take, had herded up the restaurant employees and taken them downtown for questioning. Both Thompson and Jake felt certain one of them would give up Ramirez. No doubt about it— thanks to Brianne, they were *this* close to nailing the ringleader.

But Jake was beyond furious that she'd taken the

risk and had no intention of letting up on her until she understood the gamble she'd taken and the peril she could have put herself in. For a woman who'd suffered a childhood fear of risk and sought to back away from people who thrived on the same, she had done something shocking. But knowing how Brianne had always taken control of her life, he realized now that he shouldn't have been surprised—just pissed at himself for not outthinking her first. Now he'd settle for dimming her enthusiasm.

Norton trotted beside them into the kitchen. Happy to see Brianne, he made himself her permanent shadow. "Good thing I got the doorman to take care of his walks," Jake muttered. He was in no mood to take the dog out to do business now.

"You're still upset." Brianne walked ahead of him and tossed her bag onto the table, then whirled to face him.

He held on to his composure by a slender thread. "Why would I be upset?" he asked with thinly veiled sarcasm.

Her green eyes met his. "I can think of a number of reasons."

"So can I. For one thing I had to relinquish control of questioning the employees to Duke and Vickers." But that was the least of his concerns, he acknowledged silently.

"I heard Lieutenant Thompson say that without a physical you weren't going anywhere near this case again," she said softly.

"Well, I can blame myself for that," Jake said bitterly.

When he'd set out to rehabilitate in private, he'd known he was risking the official part of the job. Since in his gut he knew he hadn't wanted to return, he'd thought the undercover work he'd accomplish in private would be worth it. But he hadn't figured Brianne's blasted independence into the equation. He hadn't thought he'd need to.

"I can let them know how good you're doing. How I think you could pass a basic physical."

"Could I?" Their therapy sessions had been minimal. They'd opted instead for personal time.

"Let's face it, Jake. Your shoulder's doing better than I thought. You don't really need private, daily therapy. I can help quicken your path back to work." She offered him the solution with hope shining in her eyes. "I'd do that for you, no matter how I feel about your putting yourself in danger."

He didn't want her in danger, either, but she didn't seem to comprehend that. But he recognized her selfless offer and he groaned. He didn't want his feelings for her to soften. Not while he was still justifiably angry.

"Thanks for the offer, but no thanks."

He didn't need her help getting him back on a job he didn't want. It was just the Ramirez case he'd needed closure on.

"Suit yourself." Brianne moved closer.

His sister had a huge penthouse with Lord knows how many rooms, but the kitchen was too small to hold Jake and Brianne. Not without a lot of sexual awareness flowing between them, anyway. She took another step toward him. He held his ground but he wasn't happy. Her strawberry scent hit him like a punch in the gut.

So did her pleading words. "Don't be angry with

me, Jake. I didn't get hurt and I knew what I was doing. I had a plan, I had pepper spray—''

"Which would have done you a lot of good when facing a drug-dealing cop killer!" His stomach turned over, and he gripped the nearest chair with both hands.

Her eyes blazed bright, alive with the knowledge of a job well done and a sense of accomplishment. Jake ought to know. He recognized what she was feeling, having experienced the rush often himself. If he'd thought he had a chance of making her see reason, she'd killed that hope.

"Do me a favor?" he asked.

Her eyebrows lifted in question.

"Keep quiet. Because every time you speak, you make things worse, not better."

A muscle ticked in her jaw. "You're one to talk. You're the one who's willing to make yourself a walking target for Ramirez. Now you're angry I did the same?"

"You're damn right I'm angry. If I'd gone after Ramirez, I'd have been doing my job. You were an inexperienced civilian ducking out on a bodyguard hired to protect you." He forcibly stopped himself from pointing his finger at her or reacting in any other physical way.

But he realized he was yelling and took a step back. His behind hit the counter, and he found himself trapped between the cabinets and her lush body. A body he wanted even now, despite—or was it because of—the heated argument.

Apparently unaware she was crossing a boundary, she pointed her finger at him. "You're on leave."

That she didn't hesitate to remind him or incite his anger further told him much about her current state of mind. She wasn't falling back into trembling or fear. She wasn't having an anxiety attack. She was enjoying herself—both catching Ramirez and arguing with Jake.

Jake had to admit that a part of him was enjoying it, too. And he was turned on by her strength as well as her beauty. However, he was still angry and needed her to understand the seriousness of her situation. Now that they'd closed down Ramirez's shop, the dealer would feel cornered. He wouldn't know which of his flunkies was rolling over on him, or who he could trust.

Ramirez would have no qualms about lashing out, especially at the cops, and at Jake—which meant Brianne had to be careful. The lieutenant had doubled the protection on Frank's family, and he'd agreed to have Rina checked out in Italy to be certain. That left Brianne. She had to accept backup. She couldn't run off on her own again, and Jake intended to make that clear.

But the ringing of the telephone prevented him from speaking. He reached for it. "Lowell."

"It's Vickers."

Brianne glanced at Jake and mouthed, *Who is it?*

He raised one silencing finger in the air. "I'm listening," he said.

"The chef turned on Ramirez. We got his statement and the address of his new lab. Then just as we're ready to go on down there, Ramirez calls us. Says he'll turn himself in."

Jake was suspicious. "What's the catch?"

"You're it, buddy. He wants you in residence. Says he won't risk walking toward us while you put a bullet in his back."

Only a coward would shoot someone in the back, Jake thought. And only a coward would worry about someone doing it to him. "I'm there," he told Vickers, and hung up.

Jake turned to Brianne. "I have to go to the station."

She nodded. "Ramirez?" she asked.

"Yes." For a split second, he saw a hint of the old fear in her eyes before she quickly masked it. But her determination to fight her fear and her proven willingness to take chances led him to the conclusion that he couldn't trust her on her own. Not without a promise in return.

"What's going on exactly?" she asked.

"Give me a minute."

"Okay." She nodded, wary but willing.

Brianne lowered herself into the kitchen chair, while he disappeared out the doorway. She figured he had some things to get from his room, and that was fine. She started to bite her nails, something she'd never done before, while she sought to figure out a way to get him to either tell her what was going on or take her along with him.

He returned, looking sexy and all male in his faded denim jeans and a black T. She jumped up from her seat and grabbed his arm.

"Relax, okay? I'll be back in a little while."

His words did little to calm her nerves, but she sat back down. "Where are you going?"

He narrowed his gaze. "If I tell you, will you promise to sit tight while I'm gone?"

She let out a huge sigh of frustration, knowing she could do no such thing. "How can I promise when I don't know what you're going to tell me?"

"Brianne, please make this easy on me. I'll tell you the truth and you'll promise to stay here where it's safe." He pinned her with those gorgeous eyes—eyes that were pleading.

She wanted to agree and knew that she couldn't. If he was so desperate to extract this promise, she felt certain he was going to put himself in danger. There was no way she could sit around and wait while he did. "Tell me where you're going and let me judge for myself whether or not I can make that promise."

He rubbed his neck. "Ramirez is going to turn himself in. I'm going downtown to meet him."

She was surprised that Ramirez would give up so easily and shocked that Jake had entrusted her with his destination. And then his words sunk in. "You're going to the station? I thought you were on leave and forbidden from going anywhere near the wrap-up of this case."

He rolled his eyes. "Dammit, did you have to be so smart? I don't have time for this. Ramirez wants me there when he turns himself in." He leaned over her, obviously taking advantage of his size and making use of police intimidation tactics. "Now promise me you'll stay put till I get back."

"No." She wouldn't let herself be bullied any more than she'd let him walk into danger alone.

"I don't know when you developed this stubborn streak…"

"I've always had it. When I love someone, I stick by them. Just ask Marc."

His eyes opened wide but he didn't say anything, and Brianne refused to take back the words she'd tossed out. They weren't careless or spoken in haste.

She meant them and saying them aloud confirmed her feelings.

"Take me with you." Her pulse pounded out a rapid beat.

"No. Last chance, Brianne. Promise me you won't leave, and I promise I'll be back soon."

They were at a stalemate. "I want to but I can't." She grabbed on to the chair and started to rise. "Please understand."

"I hope you do," he muttered under his breath, and reached behind him. "Because I can't risk something happening to you, like what happened to Frank."

His dead partner, Brianne thought. And the next thing she knew Jake had snapped a pair of handcuffs around her wrist and shackled her other hand to the chair. Her gaze darted in disbelief between the cuffs and his pained face. "You wouldn't." But he just had.

"You left me no choice. You've already proven you'll go off half-cocked if left alone. If you'd promised, I'd have taken your word." He held his hand out in front of her in complete supplication.

He picked his keys up off the table and flicked on the small television in the kitchen, then handed her the remote control. He walked out, only to return a second later with a magazine that he placed in front of her on the table. "I'm sorry, but you gave me no choice."

"Tell it to someone who cares," she muttered.

She watched him leave, and betrayal lay like lead in her stomach. Brianne didn't give a damn that he obviously felt bad or that he'd apologized. She also didn't give a fig that she'd brought this on herself by refusing to promise.

If she had, she would have been lying, and she refused to lie to Jake. She yanked hard, but the metal cuffs were attached to a metal chair and neither would budge. Furious, she grabbed the magazine and began flipping through it, not really paying attention to what she saw. But when the minutes ticked by and Brianne realized he wasn't coming back, she had no choice but to settle in for the duration.

From the mailing label on the front, Brianne knew the magazine belonged to Rina, and she hoped for some interesting reading. She glanced at the television. Trashy talk shows weren't going to be enough of a distraction. She swallowed over the pain in her throat.

She crossed her legs and began to flip through the pages once more, stopping only when she reached the article entitled, "Sexy City Nights." "Lovers in New York City." "Hot Spots, Hot Nights, Hotter Sheets." Brianne laughed despite herself, but when she caught a glimpse of the photos, she stopped and looked closer. In the first, dusk was setting around a couple outside an ice-cream shop, and memories of Brianne's night at Peppermint Park with Jake came flooding back into her mind.

When she thought of that night, it wasn't the sex that stood out, although it had been incredible. And it wasn't the dessert, although the rich treat had been delicious. What stood out was how hard Jake had tried to pick a place that would mean something to her. How he'd attempted to give back what she'd been deprived of in the past. And how he'd believed her when she'd questioned him about being followed. He may not have revealed his suspicions, but he hadn't discounted hers, either. Not the way her parents had, way back when.

Because he cared.

Not that his caring meant she'd forgiven him for

cuffing her to this damn chair, but if his reasons mirrored hers for walking into The Eclectic Eatery in the first place, she could begin to understand.

Caring. Love. A future? All things she now knew she wanted. She couldn't stand by and watch him walk out of her life without a fight. Losing him that way wouldn't be as bad as losing him to a bullet—because he'd be alive—but he was worth fighting for. *They* were worth fighting for. She realized now that she could live with his risky life because she didn't want to live without him. Not if she had a choice.

She studied the pictures on her lap. Interesting, erotic images of ecstasy. Without warning, Norton lifted his head and stood, then began barking and bolted for the other room.

"Traitor," she muttered. "Jake?" she called. She rose and started to walk, but the chair and the cuffs held her back. "You're going to pay for this," she yelled out in frustration.

She heard the heavy tread of footsteps coming toward the kitchen. "Come uncuff me, will you?" Then maybe she could work on the forgiving angle. Maybe.

"My pleasure."

Brianne turned toward the open doorway of the room in time to put a face to the voice—the accented voice of a man who couldn't be anyone other than Louis Ramirez.

# 12

HE'D ACTUALLY HANDCUFFED Brianne. And guilt lay like lead in Jake's stomach. He took the elevator down to the lobby. He waved to the doorman who followed him out, holding the door open as he exited the building. Jake turned right at the corner and headed for the subway, but the entire time his conscience and his heart told him to go back. So did the niggling in his brain that had begun when Vickers called and told him Ramirez was turning himself in.

Jake shook his head at his thoughts. He was just preoccupied with Brianne, as usual looking for any excuse to put her before this case. He couldn't believe she wouldn't do something as simple as promising him she'd sit tight. And he reminded himself she wouldn't be tied up now if he'd been able to trust her. Stubborn, headstrong woman. She'd already proven she'd take dangerous risks, given the right incentive.

The right incentive. Jake paused at the top of the steps leading down to the subway. *When I love someone, I stick by them.* Her words came back to him—Brianne's incentive for making that trip to The Eclectic Eatery. *When I love someone...*

His heart squeezed tight in his chest, and Jake slapped his hand against the hard metal railing. How the hell had he let those words slip by him unnoticed? Because for the first time since meeting Brianne, he'd been a cop before a man. A detective before the man who loved her in return.

He'd turned a deaf ear to her words and her pleas. He'd cuffed her to a chair and left her alone…so he could watch Ramirez walk himself into a police station and willingly give up?

Not likely. Jake shook his head as reality reared its head. There wasn't a chance in hell Ramirez would willingly admit defeat and surrender. No possibility at all. Which meant…the phone call to the cops had been a setup.

"Shit." Jake turned and hit the street at a dead run. He only hoped he wasn't too late.

A few minutes, but what felt like hours later, he reentered the building—and the doorman was nowhere in sight. A quick glance behind the desk confirmed Jake's worst fears. The man lay in a crumpled heap on the floor. The *whoosh* of revolving doors sounded in his ear, and he turned around in time to see an unfamiliar couple walk in the door.

"Where's Harry?" the woman asked.

Jake didn't think she'd like his answer, so he dug into his pocket and flashed his badge instead—a move that stopped both people cold and had them exchanging wary glances.

Jake reached behind the desk for the telephone and pulled it onto the high counter. "Call 911. Give the police the address and tell them it's the penthouse," Jake called over his shoulder as he ran for the elevator.

During the silent ride up to the apartment, Jake's life passed in front of his eyes. It was a cliché he'd heard other cops describe, but it was real. And everything he saw, everything he wanted now and in the future, included Brianne—if Ramirez hadn't hurt or killed her already, he thought fearfully.

Moving on autopilot, he removed his sneakers in order to maintain the element of surprise. He positioned himself flat against the side of the enclosed area, a place that he hoped hid him from immediate view. At last, the elevator doors slid open. A quick glance told him Brianne and Ramirez weren't in the open entryway.

Gun in hand, he crept silently into the apartment. He knew better than to call out, but damn he wished he knew where to check first. Though he'd left Brianne in the kitchen, it seemed unlikely Ramirez would keep her in the open, unlocked room. Then again, he'd have to move both Brianne and her chair, something Jake knew Brianne wouldn't allow. Not without a kicking, screaming fight.

He started toward the kitchen, just as Norton ran into the room, doing his infamous run-and-skid routine. The dog normally saved the bit for Brianne. Norton being happy to see Jake when Brianne was around was unusual, and the knot in Jake's stomach tightened.

He knelt down beside the excited dog. "Come on, boy. Where is she?" he whispered.

Norton nudged Jake's leg and started running. Jake mentally took back any bad thing he'd ever said or thought about the dog. In Jake's book, loyalty to Brianne counted for everything. The dog led him to the kitchen. As Jake got closer, he heard the sounds of a scuffle.

No matter how much he wanted to storm into the room, he had to know what was going on first. Jake paused alongside the wall to the left of the entry and looked around the corner and into the room where he'd left Brianne. He nearly lost control at what he saw.

Ramirez loomed over Brianne. Her blouse was torn, and Ramirez rested his hand, which held a gun, on her shoulder, while his free hand hovered over her breast. Fury and a possessiveness unlike any he'd ever known ripped through Jake, but the other man's gun kept him silent. He knew he didn't have a clear shot at Ramirez as long as the thug stood in front of Brianne.

Taking a gamble, Jake walked into plain view and leveled his gun at the other man. "Let her go, Louis."

Ramirez rose to his full height and turned, but kept his weapon on Brianne's shoulder, aimed at her head. "Welcome home, Detective."

Jake's aim didn't falter, either. "Drop the gun."

"As if you're in any position to be giving orders." A smirk pasted on his face, Louis cocked his weapon.

The noise echoed loudly in the room and even louder in Jake's head. At the offending sound, the blood drained out of Brianne's face. Her green eyes were wide, yet, at a glance, he saw the hidden strength he'd always known she possessed.

*Hang in there.* He tried to communicate silent support and a promise. He'd gotten her into this. He'd get her out. His heart rose in his chest, making his throat as raw as his emotions. He couldn't lose her.

And he wouldn't, Jake thought, immediately shifting his stare back to Ramirez.

"This is between us. Leave her out of it."

"He sent me flowers, remember, Jake? I think that makes me part of things," Brianne said.

Jake muttered a curse and started to sweat. He didn't know what she was up to, but her odds of escaping safely rose only if she kept her mouth shut. He didn't want her trying to elicit a confession or making herself even more expendable in Ramirez's eyes. At this point, they'd have Ramirez on a good number of charges. Jake couldn't give a damn about the drugs. All he wanted was an easy shot that didn't put Brianne at risk of taking a bullet at the same time.

"Beautiful flowers for a beautiful woman. Did you like them? It galls me to admit it, but you've got taste, Lowell. I wanted a bite for myself." He ran the butt of the gun down Brianne's cheek, and she stiffened in her seat. "It's a pity I'm going to have to miss out. Screwing her would have been screwing you at the same time." Ramirez laughed, the chilling sound a knife in Jake's gut.

Brianne shuddered with a revulsion she couldn't hide.

"Come on, Louis," Jake said. "If you kill another cop, you won't walk on a technicality this time." And if he killed Brianne, Jake would make sure he took Ramirez out before going down himself.

"I wouldn't be so sure," Ramirez said.

Brianne glanced at Jake and silently implored him not to do something rash. She knew he longed for a deadly shot at Ramirez. One that would end things for good. She swallowed over the lump in her throat and refused to look down at her torn shirt.

But she knew, as if she could read his mind, that he blamed himself for her situation. He believed she sat in this chair with Ramirez holding a gun to her head because Jake had cuffed her and disappeared.

She couldn't tell him now and might never get the chance, but she forgave him. Whether or not he loved her the way she loved him—and the jury was still out on that one since he'd had no reaction to her declaration earlier—she wouldn't hold it against him. She understood that she'd cornered him until he had no choice but to protect her from herself.

He met her gaze again, and, in those brief moments, Brianne felt an unspoken shift in their relationship. An acknowledgment of emotion that would have to be dealt with—if they got out of this alive.

She gripped the seat of the chair with one hand; the other one was still cuffed to the chair and sore from being held back in an unnatural position. But Ramirez wasn't allowing her any leeway.

"What about the guard you decked downstairs?" Jake asked, and Brianne realized Jake was trying to keep Ramirez talking and not shooting.

Ramirez shrugged as if the injured man were of no consequence. "How can anyone explain what a burned-out cop will do when he loses it?" he asked.

"You think the cops'll blame me?"

Brianne remembered her self-defense class and gauged the angle from the bottom of her foot to Ramirez's groin, but she still didn't have a good target. And neither did Jake. Ramirez stood too close, partially blocking Brianne and definitely able to get a round off if Jake fired first. She wanted to cry in frustration.

"Ask me if I care," Ramirez said. "As long as they can't trace me to this apartment I'm fine."

And he wore clear rubber gloves to make sure he got away clean, Brianne noticed. She looked around for a way out and saw Norton pacing by Jake's feet. The dog had been agitated since Ramirez's arrival, but he was no threat and the man obviously knew it because he'd left Norton unharmed. Thank God. But threat or not, the dog was definitely a potential distraction.

She tried to calculate the last time he'd been outside to do business and couldn't remember. Her mind was too muddled with fear. Anxiety was only a breath away. Her breathing came in orderly succession only by sheer force of will. She couldn't afford to become light-headed or pass out.

She glanced at the pooch and prayed Norton was in a complying mood. Brianne cleared her throat. Just as she hoped, the noise got the dog's attention and he bounded from behind Jake, coming up in front of her and Ramirez.

"Get the damn dog out of here," Ramirez said, but never dropped his weapon from its perch on her shoulder. "Before I shoot him myself."

"No!" Realizing she'd yelled at the man holding a gun, she cringed. "I mean, please don't. He's harmless, okay?" She watched the dog pace in nervous circles at their feet. "He's just doing his job. I mean, Norton does his business. He thinks he's protecting me, don't you, boy? He's just doing business."

Brianne met Jake's stunned gaze and realized he understood what she was up to. *Please don't let him get hurt,* Brianne prayed silently because she'd never forgive herself if anything happened to the dog because of her.

"Enough talking!" Ramirez said, glancing back and forth between them. "It's time to get this over with."

And just as he spoke, Norton did what Rina had trained him to do. He lifted his leg and did his business on Louis Ramirez's leg and shoes.

Ramirez glanced down, and fury filled his already

hate-filled face. "Fucking dog." He jumped back and kicked out his leg to get Norton away.

In the split second the gun wasn't trained on Brianne, she leaned back, lifted her foot and kicked Ramirez in the groin. The force of the movement toppled her chair backward. When her head hit the floor, she thought she heard the sound of a gunshot rent the air. Jake's gun? Ramirez's?

She didn't know, and from her awkward angle, she couldn't see. She attempted to roll and lift herself up, but her arm was caught at an awkward angle; if she moved, she was afraid she'd break it. Her heart pounded in her chest, and Brianne shut her eyes tight, praying that the next voice she heard would be Jake's and not Ramirez's.

"Brianne?"

*Jake.* Emotion swept through her as quickly as the bullet had flown through the air. "Are you okay?"

He didn't have a chance to answer. A herd of footsteps sounded from across the apartment, and, within seconds, the room filled with police.

"I WANT BOTH of you downtown first thing tomorrow morning, you understand?" Thompson ordered.

"Yes, sir." Jake glanced over his lieutenant's shoulder at Brianne.

She stood in front of the high windows in the living room overlooking the city. She'd picked up Norton and perched him on the wide windowsill and was running a hand over his head. Wasn't that like Brianne? Reassuring the dog when no doubt she was in need of reassurance herself.

Jake hadn't had a word alone with her since the cavalry had arrived. He wasn't sure why Thompson was giving him the night's reprieve before taking statements, but he had a hunch the older man's soft spot was showing.

"Why are you being such a human being about this, Lieutenant?" *This* being both Jake's need to be alone with Brianne and Thompson's unspoken understanding that Jake had officially quit the force.

The Ramirez case was over. Unable to walk, Louis had been taken out of the penthouse on a stretcher, after being read his rights with no error. Accompanied by Duke and Vickers, he was on his way to the hospital, courtesy of Jake's bullet. When Brianne and Norton had made their move, Jake had had milliseconds to push the memory of the man's hands on Brianne out of his head, and take his one shot. Ramirez had dropped before he knew what hit him.

But a lot had happened since then, Jake thought. Recalling the tense minutes in the kitchen, every nerve in Jake's body now screamed for release—the kind of release only Brianne could provide. But she hadn't said two words to him since, and, though he'd like to blame her silence on the commotion following the police raid, he had a gut feeling she was still furious over the handcuffing incident.

"Shit, Lowell. You're not listening to a damn thing I have to say," the lieutenant muttered, his gaze settling behind him on Brianne.

"Maybe because she's better looking than you are, sir." Jake grinned despite the uncertainty surrounding his future with Brianne.

The lieutenant frowned, but Jake saw the humor there as well.

"Ten o'clock tomorrow, Lowell." Thompson left, taking the rest of the cops with him.

The kitchen was a shambles, taped off for further investigation. Nothing needed Jake's attention now, except Brianne. Nothing and no one else was more important.

But when the elevator doors slid shut and they were alone, words failed him. What did he say to the woman he loved? He'd left her alone and defenseless, at the mercy of a cop killer. He wouldn't blame her if she still wanted to join her brother in California and put Jake and their entire summer interlude behind her. But he planned to do his damnedest to talk her out of it.

BRIANNE FELT JAKE come up behind her. He was warm and masculine and overpowering in his intensity. But he didn't frighten her. Not even after the episode with Ramirez.

She picked up the forty-pound lug of a dog and placed him on the floor before turning to Jake.

"I'm sorry." His voice was gruff with emotion.

"I forgive you." She stood with her hands behind her, her eyes meeting his serious, penitent ones. "I even understand why you felt you had to do it." She shook her head and laughed wryly. "Like you said, it's not like I gave you a choice."

He inclined his head, his eyebrows lifted in surprise. "That's pretty generous considering you never bargained for this when you accepted Rina's job offer and place to live."

"Life's full of surprises. I learned that young."

"And you wanted nothing more than to banish those surprises in favor of a little stability." He brushed a lock of hair out of her face, his callused fingers lightly abrading her skin.

A tingle of sexual awareness started immediately. She wasn't shocked. There were few things in life she could count on, but Jake and their overwhelming chemistry were two of them.

"I think I had a naive view of the world." It was something Brianne had discovered since moving into the penthouse and becoming a part of Jake's life.

"I take it I've broadened your horizons?" A crooked smile touched his lips—lips she longed to kiss and possess, but not just yet. There was too much unspoken between them.

"You broadened them all right, in ways I never imagined."

And probably hadn't wanted to, Jake thought. Fear gripped his heart as he composed his next thought. He didn't want to put ideas in her head but he needed to lay things on the line, and soon. He couldn't take the uncertainty, not where Brianne was concerned. "I'm surprised your bags aren't packed and ready to go."

She swallowed hard. "Is that what you want? For me to leave?" Her green eyes were huge, and she seemed to back away, closer to the window—farther from him, when he wanted nothing more than to be as close as was humanly possible.

"Hell, no."

He'd never wanted any woman as badly as he wanted Brianne, never wanted any future as badly as he wanted one with her. And he'd never had so much to lose before. His heart beat out a rapid rhythm.

"That's not really telling me much, Jake. You don't want me to go now or you don't want me to go—"

"Ever."

She bit her lower lip, watching him warily. She'd heard the word, but she obviously didn't believe him.

"You said you weren't looking for a long-term relationship."

He grinned, feeling on stronger ground. "You said it first. I thought it prudent to agree. I probably meant it—at the time. But then, you said you wanted to move to California."

She nodded. "I said it and I meant it—at the time." Her smile grew wider, matching his. "Marc is old enough to go without me. He never wanted his big sister going along, anyway."

As long as he'd pushed this far, Jake figured he might as well go all the way. "You don't want a life with someone who takes risks."

She glanced down. "I don't. I don't want a relationship with someone who'll put himself in danger for the fun of it, who puts risk above his feelings for me."

Jake held his breath. For all the light teasing, he knew this subject was deadly serious. His future with Brianne hinged on her answer, for as much as he loved her, being a detective *of some sort* was in his blood.

He might forgo law enforcement in favor of becoming a private investigator—something he'd considered after hiring David. His career wouldn't change, no matter who he answered to. Brianne had to accept that. She had to accept and be able to live with him or—

"I watched you with Ramirez today." Her soft voice cut off his thoughts. "You never acted foolishly or without thought. You never tempted Ramirez to take a shot at you instead of me, not even when you walked in and found him tearing at my...blouse." She choked over the word and the memory.

He grabbed her forearms and his thumbs stroked her soft flesh, wanting to replace the bad memories with more pleasant ones. "But I wanted to. I wanted to shoot first and question him later. I wanted to throttle him with my bare hands, choke the life out of him and then shoot him again for good measure."

A sheen of moisture filled her eyes. "But you didn't and that proved something to me. Something I should have known about you all along."

"What's that?" He tipped his head down and their foreheads met and touched.

"You aren't in it for kicks. Whatever you do, it's justified and honorable. I can live with that." She stared up at him. "If you want me to."

*If he wanted her to.* Jake shook his head and looked at the woman who held his heart in her hands. The irony was, she didn't even know it. "Sweetheart..."

Brianne held her breath. She'd laid her heart out to him again, only this time Jake didn't have any place to run off to. No excuse not to answer. The grim look on his face didn't bode well for her hopes and dreams, but she forced herself to meet this last challenge with her head held high.

She'd deal with the pain of losing Jake when she was alone. After all, she'd agreed to a short-term affair. It was unfair of her to change the rules now.

She'd reached the point of no return, though, Brianne thought. Or maybe that had come the night Rina made her generous, albeit manipulative, offer. The woman had altered the course of Brianne's life. She now had both frightening and wonderful memories that she'd have to learn to live with. Even if memories were all she had.

"What is it, Jake?"

He ran a hand through his already messed hair. "I live in a one-bedroom apartment on the West Side."

That wasn't the response she'd expected, and she narrowed her eyes in confusion.

"Between us, we can probably afford two bedrooms, unless, of course, you want to move out of the city. Or if your heart is really set on California, once Rina's back and I know she's okay, we can consider that, too."

Brianne laughed, her heart suddenly lighter than any time in recent memory. "The only thing I'm understanding in that sentence is the word *we*. And after all that's happened, I'll take it."

He grinned and wrapped his arms around her neck, holding her tight. "I love you." He nuzzled his face into the side of her neck, his breath warm on her skin.

Brianne's heart was full. She had all the security and love she'd ever wanted in life. "What about that family you once wanted?" she asked a little breathlessly.

"Sweetheart, I want that more than anything. With you. And if we happened to miss that time in the whirlpool, I'm more than willing to start trying right now. I love you," he said again, his lips hot and moist against her neck. "I should have told you before I walked out earlier."

She swallowed over the lump in her throat. "I love you, too. I always have and I always will."

"I'm sorry I cuffed you." His hand slipped beneath the new shirt she'd changed into after the police had freed her, and slid over her back in a hot caress.

"How sorry?" She tilted her head back and smiled coyly.

Jake didn't miss the mischievous glint in her gorgeous eyes. "How sorry do you want me?"

She brought her hand out from behind her and dangled his handcuffs in front of him. ''I want you contrite. I want you shackled.'' Her eyes darkened to a stormy green. ''But most of all, I want you mine.''

# *Epilogue*

RINA STRETCHED her feet out in front of her in the first-class cabin. She toed off the new designer sandals she hadn't needed to buy and lifted the glass of Perrier the flight attendant had given her prior to takeoff. As she took a sip of the bottled water, she wondered why regular tap water was something the wealthy disdained, along with honesty and frank talk. Thank God, she was going home.

Mixed emotions flooded her at the thought of returning to New York and the mausoleum of an apartment she'd left behind. Though she'd never admit it to her know-it-all older brother, he was right. The place was a palace and it had only been her home when Richard was there, filling it with warmth. Now the penthouse was as cold as her husband's body.

Rina shivered but refused to shy away from the truth. After all, this trip had been as much about recovery as self-discovery. She pulled a sheet of paper from her purse. "Number one, list penthouse with Realtor," she wrote. Satisfaction replaced the yawning emptiness. She'd taken the first step toward a new life.

Just like her brother had, thanks to her. When she'd hired Brianne Nelson as Jake's physical therapist, she'd hoped she'd be giving them both a summer of fun. *Sex* and fun, she amended. Even if Rina was in mourning, that didn't mean Jake had to be. Only a statue could have missed the sexual tension humming in the air around Brianne and Jake, but neither of them had had the guts to act on the attraction. Enough was enough. She'd planned to hook them up for a sexual diversion, but after meeting Brianne, Rina had hoped that her stubborn brother wouldn't blow it and that the two of them would end up together, for good. Rina knew better than to say or think "forever."

She'd been down that foolish road once before, when she'd met Richard. But since his accident, the blinders were off. Only fate knew how long two people would have together, which was why she was grateful her plan for her brother and Brianne had worked. They were waiting for Rina's return to get married, and she knew without a doubt her brother had chosen right this time.

As for herself, Rina had done a lot of soul searching while she was gone. The money Richard had left her would keep her in luxury for the rest of her life, but what would keep her happy and sane?

Living off Richard's wealth and sitting idle would lead to boredom, and that would kill her. Her parents had instilled a strong work ethic in their kids. Because he'd seemed to want a stay-at-home wife, Rina had complied—and enjoyed it in the beginning. But boredom had set in and, thanks to the fact that she didn't need to work, she'd begun talking about starting a new career. Before she married, Rina had always wanted to write, but because freelancing articles for magazines wouldn't pay the bills, and her job left her too tired at night, she'd never made the attempt. Richard had humored her talk of writing, treating it as a whim that would pass. He'd never taken her seriously. Not since he'd swept her off her feet, out of his office and into his bed.

She had adored him. But she wondered what kind of future they would have had once she let him see how tired she'd grown of doing nothing except waiting for him to come home. Guilt swamped her at the traitorous thought, at the admission that her marriage hadn't been the blissful state she'd pretended it to be. But she forced herself to acknowledge that, much as he'd loved her, too, he hadn't understood her. How could he when they'd come from two different worlds?

Then again, didn't all men and women come at life from different perspectives? she wondered, thinking of Brianne and Jake. Rina flipped her paper over and started making notes, her pen moving quickly over the page. Question: What did men want? Answer: A woman. Question: What kind of woman?

In short, Rina wondered, what turned a man on? Excitement grew inside her, and she knew she had the makings of her first story. But first she'd have to do the research…

# LOOK FOR OUR EXCITING

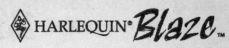

## RED-HOT READS
## NEXT MONTH!

JUST A LITTLE SEX… by Miranda Lee
SLEEPING WITH THE ENEMY by Jamie Denton
THE WILD SIDE by Isabel Sharpe
HEAT WAVES by Janelle Denison

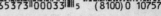

# HARLEQUIN®
*Makes any time special* ®

Visit us at www.tryblaze.com                    HBUSCOUPONSEPT

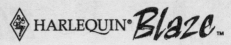

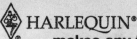

# COMING SOON...

AN EXCITING
OPPORTUNITY TO SAVE
ON THE PURCHASE OF
HARLEQUIN AND
SILHOUETTE BOOKS!

*DETAILS TO FOLLOW
IN OCTOBER 2001!*

*YOU WON'T WANT TO MISS IT!*

PHQ401